A Good Girl with Bad Habits 2

Joi Miner

A Good Girl with Bad Habits 2

ISBN 978-0692737576

Table of Contents

Imani had another night of tossing and turning. She'd gone to bed early, around eight, and planned to catch up on some well-needed rest. She was on a mission again. Knowing that she had a baby on the way motivated her to get as many extra hours at work as she could stand. She'd taken the evening off from everything: Zi, writing, TV, work. It was a well-needed break. Calling it an early night, Imani had given herself a bubble bath, listened to some Sade, and laid it down. But for some reason she couldn't sleep. She'd doze off and then jerk back out when a nightmare crept up on her eyelids' screen.

With her belly growing, she already had a hard enough time sleeping comfortably. The nightmares didn't help. Her raised heartbeat would wake the baby inside of her and she'd start kicking uncontrollably. Nights like this, she really wanted to call Vincent and lay against his comforting chest and strong arms, she knew he'd make her feel safe. She smiled thinking about Vincent and dozed into a beautiful reminiscence of their first night together, an encounter so perfect and powerful that they'd created life. She remembered her head on his chest, the scent of their lovemaking hanging in the night air.

Just as Imani had settled into her dream, her cell phone went off. She didn't want to wake up but she thought it might be Vincent on the other end.

It was Keith. He had Zi tonight, so she thought something was wrong.

"Hello?" Imani's groggy voice came over the phone.

"Hey, Imani. I was just checking on you," he had on his nice voice. It scared Imani.

"I'm... good..." Imani hesitated, "Is Zion ok?"

She was never comfortable leaving Zi with him, but the courts had granted him visitation because he'd taken those anger management courses.

"Yeah, she's fine. I just wanted to talk to you."

"About?" Imani hesitated again, caught off-guard with his words and actions.

She didn't want to be rude but with all the bickering that they'd done, she really needed to know what he wanted. Imani checked the phone. And at one in the morning.

"Well," he stammered trying to find the words, "I've been thinkin' 'bout you lately. I mean, I know we ain't gettin' back together, but we need to try and get along for Zion's sake. How about I come by later tonight, so we can talk?"

"What is Zi doing?" she asked. Keith wanted to see her and she was having a weak moment, so she bought herself some time by avoiding his question by asking one of her own.

"She's about to go spend some time with my mom."

"Oh…"

"I really think we need to talk, because as quiet as it is kept I want the best for my daughter and I know that means having a good relationship with her mother," he said.

"Okay Keith, I will hear you out, but if you come over here the wrong way, I will have you locked up," Imani said sternly.

"I'm a better man, Imani. You will see," Keith said in a sincere way.

"Aiight."

They agreed for him to come meet her after he dropped Zi off at her mom's later that day. Imani rolled back over to go try and sleep again. The baby started moving around inside her, as if trying to get comfortable. When her belly stopped shifting, Imani found a comfortable position on her left side and eased off to sleep.

Around 8:30 that evening, Imani heard a knock on the door. She looked through the peephole to see Keith's long, hairy face. He was five foot six inches in stature but his ego made him a leering six feet even.

He was standing there arrogantly, as if he was supposed to have been there. Imani was having second thoughts about opening her door. Looking at him made the hair on the back of her neck stand up. But she was lonely and he was there, so she pushed her concerns to the back of her mind.

Imani opened the door in a red, green, and yellow sarong. She'd made sarongs a large part of her wardrobe due to their comfort with her second trimester-swollen belly. She'd forgotten that she hadn't mentioned her pregnancy to him and he had no way of knowing, because he picked Zi up and dropped her off at her mom's.

Not in the mood for his insults or smug facial expressions, Imani walked back into her loft, leaving him at the door. She walked over to her couch and sat down, Indian-style, feeling a sudden urge for a Black & Mild. He stayed in her doorway for a few moments, letting what he'd just seen register. When the shock wore off, he came in, asking no questions.

He sat beside her, putting his arm around her and pulling her close. Imani had the whole mood set for easy conversation. She'd lit candles and her oil burner had the house smelling like roses. Saul Williams' She album was playing softly. Even though his words were socially relevant, his sultry voice could set any mood. Keith lifted Imani's chin so that he was looking in her eyes. He was giving her his best enticing look. But it didn't work.

Imani found herself giggling at his attempt. He smiled, embarrassed that his wooing didn't work. Not wanting to waste any more time, he kissed her. A man hadn't kissed her since Vincent last touched her, so the feeling of it caught her off-guard. She remembered a time when she was completely in love with Keith, as he slid his tongue into her mouth.

Imani reluctantly accepted his kiss. His hands slid behind her neck, untying her sarong. She let the sarong fall, revealing her swollen breasts and protruding belly.

His kisses trailed down her neck and he cupped her breasts with his hands before taking her right nipple into his mouth. He began sucking and slurping ravenously. At first it was exciting to Imani. She felt her pussy swell and get wet. Then, he put his hand in her lap and shoved his hand into her.

"Ouch. Easy," Imani was straddling the fence between being turned on and turned off.

"Mmm. You're gonna feel good. I remember how good you felt when you were pregnant with Zion," he responded, disregarding her statement altogether.

"Keith, chill out. It ain't goin' nowhere," Imani pleaded again, as he unbuckled his pants and pulled his dick through the hole in his boxers.

He pushed her back, sliding between her legs, paying no attention to her face or pleas. She tried to push him up. And he held her arms down while he shoved himself inside of her.

"Dude! Stop!" Imani yelled.

He forced his tongue into her mouth to silence her. She turned her face away and tried to wiggle free. He was hurting her and pressed his weight onto her stomach to keep her still until he finished. Imani couldn't move but her child was moving in protest to the weight and ramming. Her face was wet with tears and she hated herself for going against her better judgment.

Keith was hurting her so badly she screamed for help, hoping someone would hear her and call the police. He grabbed her around her neck, keeping his weight on her stomach. She felt herself begin to lose consciousness. But before she did, she saw the familiar look of hate in his eyes and heard him make a statement that would stay with her for the rest of her life.

"Stupid bitch," he spat in her face, "you left me to have some random niggah's baby. I'mma take care of you and this little bastard!" Imani passed out.

Rock-a-bye Baby

Rock-a-bye baby
My future you were.
Gave in to weakness
Now I won't meet him or her.

"Imani… Imani… WAKE UP!" Nia screamed, standing over her friend's limp body.

She'd called Imani to check on her and hadn't gotten an answer after her fourth call, so she decided to stop by. The door had been ajar, something Nia knew her friend wouldn't do in the neighborhood she lived in. She'd walked in to find Imani unconscious and bleeding on her couch.

"Hello… I need an ambulance," Nia called 911 from her cell phone giving them the address. "Please hurry!"

Imani came to while her friend was calling for an ambulance.

"Nia?" Imani called to her friend weakly.

Nia turned on her heels and ran across the apartment to Imani's side. "Imani! Oh thank God! What the hell happened to you?!"

Imani tried to sit up, but Nia stopped her. "You're bleeding, babe. Don't move."

"I'm bleeding?" Imani snapped out of her haze. She was concerned for her child now. She placed her hand between her legs and burst into tears as she held her bloody palm.

The EMT's arrived and transported Imani to the hospital. One of them told her that she may be having a miscarriage. Imani became hysterical. They had to sedate her and, when she came to, she was met with Nia's sullen face.

"My baby?" Imani asked, although she already knew the answer to the question.

"I'm sorry, Imani," Nia walked over and hugged her friend, "What happened to you?"

"Keith... happened... to... me," Imani stated between sobs. She told her friend the whole story, and then repeated it for the nurses and police officers after a rape exam was done.

"We'll get him, Ms. Jones," the black officer with the gentle eyes assured her. But Imani wasn't so sure. She just wanted to be left alone to mourn the loss of her child.

Before Nia left her alone for the night, Imani grabbed her hand. Between sobs, she said two words that she hadn't told anyone else.

"He knew."

****

Imani cried the two days that they kept her in the hospital. It was like she was mourning her divorce all over again. She was so excited about having this new life inside of her. She felt like she was getting a second chance. She'd had an appointment the next day to find out the sex of her child.

Guess I'll never know, she said to herself, sadly.

She'd made a mistake that had cost her the life of her child. It hurt. She tried to cheer herself up by remembering how blessed she was that Keith hadn't taken her life, too. It wasn't working. She'd just have to keep reminding herself until the sting wore off and she believed it. Imani completely understood the place people who took their own lives were in when they decided to give up. She felt like she was there now. Zion was the only thing that made her life worth living now...

****

Nia came and picked Imani up when she was released. She helped her into the house. Imani looked at her living room and saw that something was different. Nia had gotten rid of her couch and bought her a new one: a plush sofa with old-fashioned fabric and extended pillows with buttons sewn in them. Nia helped Imani sit down. She had been given time off work and used her sick leave to make sure her paycheck wasn't going to be short.

Nia offered to stay but Imani wanted to be alone. Nia promised to call and check on her later.

"You call me if you need anything," Nia urged, handing Imani the remote control and walking out the door.

Imani turned on the TV and flipped through the channels until she found an episode of Golden Girls. Tears ran down her cheeks as the women acted out their humorous scenes. Imani cried until she dozed off to sleep.

Before completely losing consciousness, Imani heard Saul Williams' voice speak to her with different meaning:

"Rise and shine my mother used to say, pulling back the clouds of covers that warmed our night. But the fleshy shadows of that moonless night stored the venom in its fangs to extinguish the sun. Rise and shine, but how can I when I have crusty cloud configurations pasted to my thighs? And snow covered mountains in my memories. They peek into my daily instruction, my moments. They hide in the corners of my smile, and in the shadows of my laughter. They've stuffed my pillows with overexposed reels of ABC afterschool specials. And the feathers of woodpeckers that bore hollows into the rings of time that now ring my eyes, and have stumped the withered trunk of who I am… I keep trying to forget, but I must remember. And gather the scattered continents of a self, once whole. Before they plant flags and boundary my destiny. Push down the watered mountains that blemish this soiled soul before the valleys of my conscience get the best of me. I'll need a passport just to simply reach the rest of me. A vaccination for a lesser god's bleak history."

"I'm sorry Vincent..." Imani mouthed into the universe, hoping he'd forgive her.

If only she'd been able to sleep that night.

****

Imani cried and slept for the next seven days. She barely ate, except for when Nia stopped by and practically force-fed her. She'd munch on peanut butter crackers and water when she started hurting and needed a Lortab. She took sitz baths with her friend's help. Nia was a godsend; she was the only person keeping Imani going. She talked to Zi every night but couldn't muster up the strength to go get her child or look into the face of her baby who carried half of the DNA of the man who'd done this to her. Imani knew, in her heart, that it wasn't Zion's fault but her heart was aching. She was mourning her unborn child and didn't want to deflect her pain and frustration onto her living child.

Halfway into her second week, Imani returned to work although her doctor had given her a pass for six weeks. She couldn't stand staring at those empty walls anymore. Moving through life like a zombie, she had to take everything step-by-step, even simple functions like walking and driving. Imani felt dead. Nothing mattered. Life became more of a routine than an experience.

Before she knew it, days turned into weeks. Her physical pain subsided. She lost her belly bulge and started to feel a little like herself again. She hadn't even realized, in her mourning, that she hadn't had any desire to be in the company of a man. She spent most of her free time writing and letting Nia try to pep her weakened spirit back to life. On the day of Imani's six-week check-up, she felt a weight weighing heavily on her shoulders. She didn't want to get up; there were a million questions running through her mind. She knew she had to get up, though, or they'd never get answered. She rolled around in her bed until the last possible minute. Nia had called a few times to make sure that Imani was up and would be ready when she came to pick her up.

Nia walked into the house to find Imani still in bed. At least she'd kicked the covers off. Nia didn't even bother turning the lights on. She tiptoed to the side of the bed where Imani lay, on her stomach with a pillow over her head, and smacked her friend on her booty.

"Get up!" Nia said laughingly.

"Ugh, Nia! You get on my nerves!" Imani rolled over and sat up on the side of her bed.

She smiled at her friend endearingly before pulling on a pair of sweat pants and a tank top. She looked at her friend's face and answered her before she asked.

"I showered last night, Nia," she stated, sounding like her child. This realization made her smile.

Sliding her feet into her Crocs, Imani followed Nia out the door of her apartment and got into the car. She said nothing all the way to her Midwife's office. Nia didn't pressure her, knowing Imani had a lot of things on her mind.

They parked and walked into the office. Imani signed in and sat in the waiting room waiting for her name to be called. She was fidgety, picking at her fingernail polish, twisting in her hair, patting her foot. Nia finally grabbed her hand to calm her. Stroking the back of Imani's hand with her thumb. When they finally made it to a room, Imani got undressed and covered herself with the paper robe the nurse had given her. After a full, and uncomfortable, check-up, she was told that she could get dressed. When her Midwife, Valerie, came back, she gave her a clean bill of health and asked Imani if she had any concerns.

"Well," Imani hesitated, taking Nia's hand, "I was wondering if I will be able to have any more children?"

Valerie smiled and gave Imani a comforting look with her big, light blue eyes.

"And why wouldn't you?" she asked rhetorically.

Imani breathed a sigh of relief. Her face softened and she smiled genuinely for the first time in months. Her smile was gone as quickly as it had come, though, as she came to the realization that she needed to call Vincent and tell him what had happened. Fighting back tears, Imani gave Valerie a hug and she paid her co-pay before leaving.

Teary-eyed, she looked out the window again, not wanting to talk. Even though some of her worries had been calmed, she still had a lot to think about. Nia refused to let her friend sulk anymore.

"See, Imani," Nia chirped excitedly as they took the exit to I-65 South heading back to Downtown from the East Side where Imani's Midwife had her office, "I told you everything was gonna be alright."

"But Nia," Imani started, fighting back sobs.

"You weren't meant to have this baby, Imani, so cut that shit out!" Nia didn't realize she was yelling. "You were doing the shit all wrong. You ran into that man's sister the day you found out you were pregnant for a reason and your stubborn ass still didn't call him and tell him what the business was. He deserved to know. He cares about you because it's been six months and he's still trying to reach out to you. You need to stop with your bullshit and give that man a chance."

Imani didn't say a word. She just stared out of the window all the way home. When they pulled into her parking lot, Imani took a deep breath when she saw Vincent, sitting on the hood of his S-10 with a dozen red roses.

"Nia?" Imani let the question hang in the air. She looked at her friend who flashed her a smile.

"I knew you weren't gonna call him, so I did," Nia said, putting the car in park.

Imani jumped out and ran into Vincent's arms. He picked her up and carried her to her apartment, putting her down so she could open the door. Imani looked back at her friend, mouthing "thank you" before they disappeared into the house.

Fall Back

Time and space heal all things
I only prayed that, in time,
Love will bring you back to me.

Vincent sat Imani down on the couch, gently. He joined her and stared off into space for a while before he spoke. Not being able to bear the silence, she spoke first.

"I went to the doctor and she told me I can still have children. We can try again, baby," she said, hoping that would ease some of his concerns.

"What the fuck was he doing over here, Imani?" he asked, throwing her off because he'd never spoken to her that way. His eyes were slits and he was livid.

"I was lonely and had a moment of weakness, baby. I didn't think…"

"You didn't think that he was gonna do the same shit he did to you for years? Really, Imani? You put yourself and our child in danger. I can't believe you!"

"Vince, hear me out. I'm so sorry," Imani plead with him.

"You're not over him, Imani. Even after all the shit he's put you through, you keep running back. I'm willing to be patient with you, but I won't chase your ass while you're running back to who broke you. I need some time. And you should take this time to get your shit together and decide what the hell you want. I don't have time for this shit."

He took the roses he'd gotten her and put them in a vase before leaving. She didn't see things going this way. She sat there in shock.

She didn't say anything, even when she saw him heading towards the door. He turned around, the doorknob in his hand.

"I love you Imani, but I need you to really think this shit through. I'm too grown to be wasting my time on someone who doesn't understand what the hell she wants for herself. But, even if you don't choose me, I realize that you and Zion deserve to be treated better than that sorry excuse for a man has, or will ever, treat you."

With that, he walked out of the door. Imani had no idea what to do. She wanted to follow him but she knew he needed space. And she really didn't know what she wanted. She didn't go into Books-a-million looking for a relationship when Vincent happened. He was a great man, but she wasn't sure if she was ready. She'd definitely take some time to think about it. She picked up her phone.

"Hey momma... I'm on my way to get Zi. I know I'm still healing but I want my child at home with me tonight. Whatever, momma. Have her ready when I get there, please."

She hung up the phone, headed to get her child. Her mom had tried that whining shit, but the way Imani was feeling, she wasn't hearing it today.

The Proposition

I'd give my life and myself for you
You're worth it.
Do whatever it takes
To give you what you deserve.

At 6 a.m., Imani woke up with her child sprawled across her chest. Their positioning resembled a cross or lowercase 't'. She rolled Zion off her and got up to make breakfast. She put on her silk robe so the grease from the bacon and eggs didn't pop her in places that would hurt terribly. She made grits, eggs, turkey bacon, and honey butter biscuits. After breakfast was done, Imani went back down the hall to begin the task of waking her child. Zion absolutely hated waking up in the morning. The child loved her sleep.

Imani jumped into the bed. Pouncing on Zi, she tickled her daughter awake. When Zion responded by swatting her mother away and rolled over, Imani began littering her with kisses. Imani could see Zion's dimples crease her cheeks as she smiled in feigned sleep.

She cracked her eyes and whispered, "Stop Mommy."

Zion sat up reluctantly, stretching to the walls and yawning. Imani told her to go to the bathroom and wash-up. They washed their faces together. Brushed their teeth. Imani left while Zion lotioned up and pulled her daughter's clothes from the closet. Today she was wearing a green, floral shirt, light blue jeans and black rain boots with peace signs all over them. Imani had pulled out a matching outfit for herself, a green and blue paisley patterned V-neck shirt, distressed blue jeans, and black high-top Chuck Taylor's with peace signs on them.

They dressed and ate breakfast. Zion told Imani about the antics of her classmates. Imani listened intently, laughing at the things children find to get into in daycare. After they ate, Imani packed Zion's lunchbox with a bologna Lunchable, two packs of fruit snacks, and Goldfish, and they were out the door.

Imani walked into the Learning Tree on Troy Highway and signed Zion in. She kissed her baby and was on her way out the door when the director, Ms. Andrews, stopped her.

"Ms. Jones," she caught her attention, "can I speak with you moment?"

Imani had a little time before work, so she followed her into her office. Ms. Andrews closed the door behind them. Imani had a seat in the chair facing the Director's paper-filled desk. Ms. Andrews took her seat behind the desk and pulled out her receipt book. She flipped to the back where there were list of names and amounts written in red ink. She looked over her glasses at Imani, folded her hands over her book, and pursed her lips.

"I stopped you today because your account with us is delinquent," she paused briefly before continuing. "The last payment was made on February 20th and we haven't received anything since. That was six weeks ago. Your ex-husband has come in, when he picks Zion up, and made promises to pay each week but hasn't yet. He told me he was the processes of getting his finances together after your divorce and that he was going to pay the balance soon. But the past two weeks, he hasn't even been here to get her, and we don't have his contact information." She stopped. Apparently, she could see the fumes rising from Imani's head.

Imani cleared her throat, trying to maintain her composure.

"So you're telling me that he hasn't been paying anything at all?" she repeated this information back to the woman.

"Yes ma'am," the director confirmed. "I hate to bring this to you in this way, but at this point, you are twelve hundred dollars in arrears, not including late fees. And since you are the one that registered her, we need you to satisfy this balance or we will be unable to keep Zion next week and I'll have to give her slot to someone else."

Imani's mind started to race. Where in the hell was she going to get that kind of money? She was beyond livid. This woman had the gall to tell her that her child couldn't come back based on the actions of her ex-husband and her fool ass not doing her job! Imani's jaw tightened as she chose her words very wisely.

"Ms. Andrews," Imani started slowly, "I apologize that you were misled by Keith, but I don't have twelve hundred dollars just sitting around. I'm recovering from a divorce from that lying sack of shit and the only thing that I got of value out of the entire five and a half years of marriage was my child. I'm angered, and very disappointed, by the fact that you allowed this situation to go on so long without saying anything to me."

"But he said..." The director interjected.

"Let me finish," Imani cut her off. "This is no way to run a business. Now, here's what's going to happen. I will pay you what's owed, less the late fees, because that was your own doing, and after next week, which I will pay for, I'll be taking my child elsewhere."

Imani stood, preparing to leave.

"Now, if you want to discuss late fees, I can give you Keith's home and cell numbers and you can take that up with him. And you can take your damn slot, and this ill-run operation, and shove it! I'll have your money on Monday. And, let me make myself clear when I say this, if there is any kind of mistreatment of my child while she's here because of your actions, I'll take that twelve hundred that I owe you out of your ass with interest!"

Imani turned on her heels and stormed out of the office and the daycare. She sat in her Escort wanting to scream. Keith had fucked her, yet again. She was so angry she had thoughts of killing him, dismembering his body and taking a cross-country trip, leaving his remains in remote locations all over the United States. She'd watched enough episodes of Snapped to pull it off, she believed. But she knew, just like the women on Snapped, she would eventually get caught.

She took a few deep breaths before pulling out of the parking lot. She fought the urge to call Keith, because she knew he was waiting on this call. She wouldn't let him win. Wouldn't let him hear the anger in her voice. There she was, faced with practicing self-control again. She had to focus on what was important. She had to figure out where in the hell she was going to get $1,200 from before Monday. She had four days and no idea. She wasn't going to call her mother or her aunt because they helped with Zion enough already. She was going to figure it out.

Before she went to work at the Auction, Imani stopped by Calvary Christian Academy. Her mother had been telling her that this was where Zion needed to be instead of daycare. She got some materials about admission costs and registration. The secretary advised her they had an opening because one student's family had just moved. The father was military and had gotten stationed in Virginia. Imani was grateful for this, but that was another $300 she was going to have to come up with. That, though, she knew her mother would help with. Maybe she could find a way to tell her, without giving all the details, that she'd decided to make the switch. Imani decided to worry about that later. Right now, she had to get to work and think of a plan to pay her daycare debt.

She pulled into a full parking lot at Deanco Auto Auction. She checked her make-up in her rearview mirror, turned on her million dollar smile, and prepared to do her part in making these auto dealers feel good about the 'great deals' they'd just gotten on the automobiles they'd just purchased. Imani loved this job. It was easy money. Flirting with rich men that she'd never give the time of day outside of the auction.

To all of these white dealers, she was exotic. Brown-skinned and natural with a wide mouth, firm body, and swayed back made her the perfect image of what they jacked off to in magazines and flicks. They'd offer to whisk her away from her job. Take her to expensive dinners. Buy her jewelry. Some even offered marriage proposals. Imani was always tickled at their advances. She didn't do pink penis, so they didn't have a chance in hell. But, Imani thought as she stood at the copier making duplicates of the sales plans for the day, today she may just make an exception for the highest bidder. She laughed to herself at the idea of tricking for daycare money. She's sure that would just make Keith's day to know she had to sell herself to get out of the debt he'd put her in purposefully.

You know what, Imani thought to herself, fuck Keith.

She would do whoever or whatever she had to so that her daughter was okay. With that thought, Imani finished up her copies and sauntered to her seat at the bottom of the first auction block. She turned on her charm full-blast, her answers to their questions about the vehicles for sales slathered with baby, honey, darlin, and sugar. The dealers, being the men that they were, were very receptive to her treatment. Some competed with one another, just to get the winning bid and have a few moments alone with her in the main office, signing paperwork. One in particular, Steve Reynolds, who owned a dealership in Tuscaloosa took full advantage of Imani's obviously open demeanor. After purchasing his sixth used car, he followed Imani into the office.

"So, can I take you to dinner tonight?" he asked as soon as they were alone.

Imani giggled. He'd been after her since she began working at the auction four months ago.

"Don't you have to get home?" Imani responded, filling out the forms.

"No, I'm actually staying in town tonight. The Biscuits are playing and I'm gonna catch the game. It would be nice to share the company a beautiful woman, too."

Imani paused and looked up from her paperwork. "What about your cars, Mr. Reynolds?"

"Call me Steve," he replied, "and my drivers can take the cars back."

Imani smiled. Avoiding answering him immediately, she turned the papers to him. "Sign and initial the highlighted areas for me, Sugar."

She handed him the pen. He held on to her hand briefly before beginning to sign off on his purchases.

"I'll make it worth your while," he lifted his eyes from the paper to make sure Imani got his message.

Imani smiled again, knowing he was dead serious. This was going a lot easier than she'd thought it would. Apparently Mr. Reynolds, Steve, was used to paying women to keep him company.

"I'll think about it," Imani responded.

She didn't want to come across as the type of woman that sold herself easily or often. But she was definitely interested. She was, however, at war with herself. He must've seen the apprehension in her face because he proceeded with reassurance.

"Look," he started, "I'm a very discrete man. What we discuss stays between us. And what we do in our personal time is our business," he paused, smiling his salesman smile. "You won't have to worry about anyone else propositioning you, either. I want to keep all of your free time for myself."

Imani blushed through her chocolate tones. This man was charming. She could see why he was so successful in his career of choice.

"Sign here for me, Mr. Reynolds... Steve," Imani continued to avoid the proposition that was now obviously sitting on the table.

Steve smiled, knowing he was that much closer to getting what he wanted. And he wanted this woman. Every slim, brown inch of her. There was something about her that'd caught his eye months ago. Something in the way she walked, sat, and handled all of the men that tried to get close to her. He'd paid close attention and today, he'd seen this beautiful Venus Fly Trap open up. He wanted what was in that opening. Wanted to see her face with those full brown lips wrapped around his dick. Watch the chocolate-vanilla swirl that would be his penetration of her. Wanted to see just how coarse her hair would feel in his hands. Wanted those long legs wrapped around his neck as he ate her, wanted to see the faces she made when she came.

There was definitely something regal about her. But there was also something edgy there. He knew that once he got her out of her place of business, she would open up into something wild. Beast-like. He wanted that beast. Wanted to tame it. To own it.

He'd extended his lure. Now, to get her to take the bait. Steve saw that he was going to have to turn on the charm even more and get Imani off the defensive. He signed the remainder of his paperwork, pausing after each initialed space or time his name was signed on the signature line, to meet eyes with her. He saw her breaking. She couldn't hide her smile, but he could tell it would take more than blushes to seal the deal. He noticed her need to maintain the control in their conversation. So he placed the ball in her court. After his final signature, he pulled out his checkbook and wrote a check for the balance of the cars he'd purchased. He then pulled out his wallet and took out three crisp one hundred dollar bills.

"Here's a tip for making this such a pleasant experience," he slid them across the desk. Imani couldn't stop herself from laughing at his directness.

"Now, Steve... Mr. Reynolds," she corrected herself to put him back in his place, "you know we can't take tips."

She laughed again and shook her head, getting up from her seat and heading to the Xerox machine.

He smiled, putting his money and his checkbook away. He'd broken down the wall. He could tell even though she'd made it her business to demote him back to formalities. He took out a business card and wrote something on the back before getting up and meeting Imani at the counter to collect his contract, receipt, and keys.

"Ms. Jones," he called to her before she could turn to walk away, possibly for good, "here's my card, in case you need a good deal on a car."

He smiled that salesman smile again and, when she accepted the card, made sure he flipped it slightly so she could see the writing on the back. He slid in a slick wink before walking away, whistling. He went to get his vehicles but felt the greatest prize he would collect on later that evening. He was pretty damn sure of it.

By Any Means Necessary

There's nothing I wouldn't do for my baby
She deserves the world
Lately, I haven't been the best to my baby girl...
But today, I'd give my heart, my soul, my body for her.

Imani finished up her work at the Auction. Her mind was on the business card Steve had given her. She'd seen the writing on the back, but hadn't looked yet to see what he'd "offered" her for her time. She continued with her open flirtations with the other dealers, but didn't allow anyone else to get as close to her as he had. When the Auction ended, Imani turned in her paperwork. She stayed to make sure everything matched up and all money from her block was accounted for.

When she was given the all-clear, she headed for her car. She opened the door and got in. The business card was burned into her thoughts. She still hadn't looked at it, and as she cranked up her car, she decided not to look at it until she got home. She wanted to give herself time to come up with an alternative to spending time with, and she was pretty sure having to have sex with, this man. She knew if the numbers on that card met her needs, it would be damn near impossible for her to resist. She thought about her options. She'd been a housewife up until January, so she'd not had time to build the employment history to qualify for a loan. And with her barely being able to make ends meet, they would look at her statements and see that she paid out almost every dime she took in. She wouldn't get ahead until she started the second job with Nia next week.

She was still paying on her car, so a title loan was out of the question and some other things like selling valuables could take more time than she had. As she drove past Capital Pawn Shop, she thought of a few things she could sell for profit, including the bridal set from her marriage to Keith. She'd planned to pass it down to Zion, but she didn't want to give her child that kind of curse.

She turned into the parking lot of her apartment complex and went into her house. She went through everything in her home of value and realized, to her embarrassment, that she didn't have much that was modern enough, or worth enough, to get her anywhere near the twelve hundred she needed for those back charges. She looked in her jewelry box's bottom compartment and took out the box that housed her bridal set. She wanted that shit out of her house. She decided she was gonna take herself to lunch, enjoy a drink, clear her head, and finally look at that damn business card. But first, she was getting rid of the rings.

Imani locked the door and got back into her car. She drove through Downtown to the Southside and went down Troy Highway to Capital Pawn Shop. When she opened the door, three smiling faces, all men, met her. Two white and one black with full bellies evident of the money that's in pawning, asked if they could help her. The closest one to her, a broad-shouldered black guy with a nametag that read 'Steve' made a beeline directly to her. Imani didn't know whether to take his name as a sign or not.

"I want to see how much I can get for this," Imani held out the ring box to him.

"Okay," he replied, leading her to the counter. "Are you trying to sell it or pawn it?"

"Sell it," Imani replied without hesitation.

"Okay. Let me look at what we have," Steve laughed to himself at Imani's quick response. That was a great bargaining sign. She obviously wanted to get rid of what was in that box. Opening it, he found a bridal set, white gold, at least four karats of princess cut diamonds.

When they made it to the counter he asked the million-dollar question, the one that would tell everything about her and her expectations. "So, what are you looking to get for it?" he asked.

"What's it worth?" Imani asked, trying to get a feel for this process.

"Well," he paused, looking at the ring set. "It's a beautiful set. But we can't give you anything near what it may have cost you when you bought it."

Imani nodded her head in understanding. She didn't expect to get much of anything for it, actually.

"How about eight hundred dollars?" Imani was starting as close as possible she actually needed. She knew there was little to no chance for getting the full value back. But maybe, just maybe, she wouldn't have to worry about what was on the back of that business card.

Steve smiled at her enthusiasm, "That's a bit more than we can pay you for this, ma'am." He pointed to the glass that stood between them. "Usually we don't make the much on jewelry. If I gave you eight hundred bucks, I would have to sell it for at least twelve hundred dollars, and the customers that come here to buy jewelry don't usually have that kind of money to spend. We have to make sure it's profitable at a reasonable price."

Imani reconsidered her offer. She looked at him and asked, "Alright, what are you thinking?"

"Hmmm," Steve contemplated, "about a hundred fifty."

Imani shook her head no. "How about six hundred?"

Steve took a moment to think about his next offer carefully. She was already down two hundred dollars. He knew she wasn't going to go as low as he was hoping to get her, with maximum resale profit in mind.

"Two-fifty."

His next offer came with confidence. He knew she wanted to get rid of the ring, and she didn't appear to be the type to shop around for better offers. She wasn't gonna give it up cheap, but this was the part of the job he loved: the bargaining game. And she was quite beautiful, so he was willing to drag this out as long as he could just so he could look at her a little longer.

Imani smiled her biggest smile. This was what he did for a living. He was going to keep playing with her until she gave in. So, game on.

Imani placed her hands on the counter's glass surface and gave him a stern glance. She made sure he understood she wasn't giving in that easily.

Steve got the message that Imani was giving him, loud and clear. He smiled in response. He liked this woman. There was something about her that made everything male in him stand-up and take notice. He wanted to give her more than cash for her ring and made sure his body language said just that.

"Five hundred," Imani stated, in response to his smile.

"Can't do it Miss…" He made the effort to get her name.

"Call me Imani," she replied. Smiling at his obvious flirtation. "What can you… do?" She was really about to lay it on now because she saw her in.

"Three hundred," he was taken aback by her gorgeous smile "That's what I can… do."

"Come on, Sugar." Imani laid on her Southern charm, "this isn't an engagement ring with diamond chips in it. This is a five karat flawless diamond bridal set. Are you seriously going to offer me a buck fifty a piece?"

Steve smiled again.

"This isn't a jewelry store either, Miss Imani," he chose his words carefully, as not to kill his chances of getting her number later, "it's a pawn shop. Work with me, Lovely."

Imani winked before giving her final offer, "Four hundred fifty dollars, and that's as low as I'm going."

Steve was impressed by her diligence, but he wasn't ready to give up yet.

"Final offer, huh?" he asked slyly, "three-fifty is mine."

Imani extended her hand, "Okay, I'm going to have to take my chances elsewhere."

Steve's mind was racing because he'd apparently underestimated her. Before he let her walk away, he was going to give it one final shot.

"Four hundred dollars. How about that?"

She stopped in thought before she left and debated whether she was willing to give him one last chance. That was closer to what she wanted than he had been since she'd walked into the building. She was close to her debt, even if she may have to resort to other avenues to cover the next week and get up the registration fees and first month's tuition for Calvary. Imani's mind wandered to the still unread business card in her pocket.

She nodded her head and took Steve's hand in her own to seal the deal.

"And your phone number," he snuck in, holding her hand longer than necessary.

"Sure," Imani replied taking a real look at him for the first time.

Her preoccupation with her situation had been a bit of a distraction. His hand swallowing hers was what first caught her attention. He was taller than she usually dated and a perfect chocolate brown. His broad nose spread slightly into his round cheeks. His beard bordered his cheeks on the outer edges, covered his chin fully, and met at the corners of his mustache. Full lips, covering teeth that were quite clean, even though they didn't touch and sat like individual xylophone keys set within pink gums. His eyes were slanted and almost too close together and he sported a well-shaped coily afro. He was cute… enough. And he may come in handy, so Imani would definitely keep in touch.

As he walked away to get the necessary paperwork, Imani noticed that his large-framed body wasn't sloppy. Aside from a bit of a belly, indicative of indulgence in beer and good eating, he was put together pretty well. Imani got a pen and receipt out of her purse, made sure there was nothing embarrassing listed in the purchase list, then turned the receipt over and wrote her name and number on the back. They completed their business and Imani handed him the now folded receipt before placing the four hundred dollars into her wallet. She gave him a flirtatious wink and walked, hips in full swing, to the door.

She felt like she was winning. Hell, she would've sold that ring set for twenty-five dollars any other day. But she had an agenda and she was that much closer to her mark. Imani turned back onto Troy Highway towards Taylor Road. She'd worked up an appetite with all of that bantering and thinking about the proposition she'd been offered earlier that day. As she drove past Zion's day care, she felt her blood boil a little and once again fought the urge to call Keith and give his ass an earful.

Instead, she called her mother and asked her to pick-up and keep her baby because she was going to be 'working late.' Her mother was happy to oblige. She loved spending time with her grandbaby and she knew there were times when the auctions had Imani working on paperwork late into the night. Imani hadn't decided whether she was going to be working late yet, but she knew it was definitely an option. She pulled up into the parking lot of Applebee's. She walked in and was greeted by a bubbly hostess named Brandi who seated her on the backside of the restaurant in a booth by the window, and took her drink order. Brandi informed her that her server, Jeremy, would be with her shortly.

Imani paged through the menu and decided on the Bourbon Street Steak and Shrimp Sizzler. She was looking at the drink menu when her server, a handsome, tan, blonde-haired man, who had to be barely over twenty-one, set a napkin and her water with lemon down on the table. He greeted her and offered to take her order. Imani placed her order, including a Top Shelf Long Island Iced Tea, showed her ID, and reached into her pocket for Steve's business card. She read all of the information on the front before setting it down flat on the table. She didn't have the nerve to flip it over yet. She'd wait on her liquid courage to arrive. She thought through the whole dilemma, trying to weigh every possible option for resolution. The offer got more and more enticing by the minute.

Imani hated borrowing money and didn't want to deal with the explanations and embarrassment that would accompany approaching either of her parents or her aunt for help. She thought of calling and threatening Keith, but she knew nothing under the sun would be able to convince him to help her with her dilemma. She wasn't going to let him know he had placed her in such a financial bind. The only other person she could think of, Nia, had her own family and bills.

Jeremy brought her drink and told her, "Your food will be out shortly."

Imani nodded before opening and inserting the straw into the tall, slender glass. She filled her mouth with the fluid, tasting the liquor instantly. This drink was just how she liked them, strong. Instead of sipping, she took big gulps, emptying half the glass in a matter of seconds. The lightheadedness took over her and she picked the card up from the table. She flipped it between her fingers like a playing card before slamming it down on the table like she was playing Bones. Her right hand rested over the card. She knew she needed to lift it and just take a look, but that was easier said than done.

It's now or never, she told herself.

Raising her hand slowly, her eyes almost bulged out of her head. She couldn't be seeing straight. On the back of the card there were three sets of words and two numbers. The first beneath the word "Tonight" and the other beneath the words "For The Weekend." At the bottom were the words "All of the Above." Playfully, beside the words, were letters of the alphabet A, B, and C. Imani rubbed her eyes, blinked four or five good times, and looked at the ink on the card again. She was waiting on it to morph into something reasonable, or for some digits to disappear. This man couldn't be serious.

Jeremy brought her food out, giving her the distraction she needed. She couldn't think straight. As much as she wanted to blame the alcohol, it wasn't the culprit. Imani sat in a trance, waiting on her food to cool to an edible temperature. All she could think about was the film Indecent Proposal with Demi Moore and Woody Harrelson. Steve wasn't offering her a million dollars, but she'd be damned if it wasn't enough to make her financial troubles go away and leave a little for her savings. Hell, it was half a year of Zion's tuition to Calvary just for the weekend. She ate and sipped her beverage in a very distracted daze. Unlike the characters in the movie, she wasn't married, and all she had to do, she admitted to herself, was what she'd been doing for free since she was fourteen years old.

But before, she had given her body for love's sake. This time it would be for cash, so this was different. Well, not really, because she loved her child and wanted the best for her. So this was for love's sake, too. Imani warred with herself mentally. She wondered what kind of sadistic, off-the-wall shit she would be asked to do for that kind of money. Her mind then drifted to the night she'd met Vincent.

Fuck, after what I'd allowed Vincent to do, handcuffs, a leather whip, or paddled ass wouldn't be such a stretch, she thought.

Imani remembered a conversation she had with Keith one night. He told her he respected prostitutes because they were honest with themselves about what they were doing.

"All these other chickens around here," he rationalized, "walking around here all high and

mighty are tricking themselves out for a few dinners and sweet nothings. Shit, at least the hoe knows what she's getting into from the jump."

Imani laughed at herself. Was she really replaying the words of the jackass that had so craftily orchestrated her entire dilemma right now? And as justification of what she was considering doing, no less.

She chewed her food slowly. Sucked down more of her drink. Accepted Jeremy's offer to get her refill.

"Goddamn it, Keith!" she said aloud, shaking her head. She knew then that she'd made her decision.

Get It On Your Back

Legs spread,
Parallel to the horizon,
We either get validation or compensation
For our sun-kissed toes.

Imani paced through her room naked. What the hell do you wear to a baseball game? And on a weekend sexual staycation?

She'd already packed a small bag. Nothing much, just toiletries and a few underwear sets. She packed a few outfits, in case they left the hotel room. She picked a red and black thong with a zipper in the front. Might as well give easy access, she laughed to herself.

Imani put on a laced red bra to match and chose a pair of fitted Capri jeans and a low-cut purple tee. She put on comfortable three-inch purple heels, grabbed her purse, overnight bag, and her keys and was out the door before her conscience kicked in. She was supposed to meet Steve at the Embassy Suites before game time so they could ride together.

She had butterflies driving down Madison Avenue. This was definitely one for the books. Imani was never nervous about dealing with the opposite sex. But this time was different. This time was for money.

What if I don't meet his expectations? she wondered insecurely. She didn't know how these things worked. Do I get it all up front? Does he pay half before and half after? What if he didn't enjoy himself? Does that make things null and void? It's not like she could sue him if he didn't pay her. Well, she would make sure to get some answers before this train left the station.

She dialed Steve's cell phone number as she pulled into a guest parking space at the hotel. She left her bag and things in the trunk and told him she'd be waiting for him in the lobby. She was at least going to get a meal and a ball game before she set foot in his hotel room. She entered the lobby and marveled at the beauty of it. The floral arrangements and peacefully pleasant paintings. The flawlessly shining floors and the colorfully upholstered lobby furniture. The beautiful fountain in the center was surrounded by plants. All of the Guest Services Personnel welcomed her loudly with shining smiles and jovial eyes. One girl, slender with shoulder-length hair and caramel skin, asked if there was anything she could assist her with in a deep, Southern accent.

Imani smiled and told her she was waiting on someone. The girl, whose shiny gold nametag read "Tiphany" smiled back and told Imani to let her know if there was anything she could do for her. Imani nodded her okay.

Imani felt so comfortable there. Everyone was so nice. It eased her worries. She may be okay if she had her rendezvous there. When Steve walked up to Imani, she was relieved. She'd been afraid she was underdressed. He had changed from his slacks and collar shirt into a coral colored polo, khaki shorts, and tan boat shoes. He had on a cologne that Imani couldn't identify immediately. But whatever it was, it was intoxicating.

Imani stood and greeted him with a hug and a nervous smile. He stood back and took full inventory of her.

"Now," he said with a smile, "we're walking to the stadium. Are you gonna be comfortable in those shoes?"

Imani laughed, appreciating his concern. "No worries, Hun. These are my walking heels."

He smiled again and offered his arm, escorting her towards the door. As they walked together, Imani began to relax. This was going to be an interesting weekend. She might as well have as much fun as possible. They walked towards Biscuit Stadium.

"You hungry," Steve asked.

"Yeah, I could definitely eat." It had been a few hours since her lunch at Applebee's.

"Good. Me, too," he said as they made a detour to Dreamland BBQ, "and I wasn't in the mood for a damn hot dog, either."

They both laughed as they walked into the restaurant and waited to be seated. Jackie, the hostess, seated them in a booth and took their drink orders. Imani ordered a Dr. Pepper and Steve a Sweet Tea. They flipped through the menu, deciding what to order without speaking. Imani was deciding the best way to address the money issue. She had no idea what on earth Steve was contemplating over there. In the midst of her thoughts, Imani realized that this was her first real date. This saddened her a bit. Steve must have seen it in her face.

"Everything okay?" he asked, genuine concern littering his face.

"Yeah, I'm fine," Imani lied, as Jackie sat their drinks down.

"This isn't any different from a real date, Imani," Steve rationalized in an attempt to comfort her.

"Oh yeah?" Imani questioned, wanting to hear what he was going to say next.

"Yes, ma'am," he paused before sharing his logic. "Women go out on dates all the time with men with a certain," he cleared his throat, choosing the right words, "economic standing. They're preparing themselves to be set up for life."

He paused again, taking a sip of his tea.

"They sleep with these men in exchange for dinners and gifts. At least you and I are coming into this with an understanding. We both know the end result, so no need to put on, you know."

Imani nodded her head, completely engrossed in his explanation. She silenced the thought in her mind that he sounded like Keith. She was going to let this salesman sell this logic to her and she was going to swallow the lump of it with a couple strong sips of her Dr. Pepper, a few beers at the Stadium, and later, shots of something strong and mind-numbing.

Jackie returned to the table and informed them that the servers were swamped. She took their food orders to 'help out'. Imani and Steve looked around at the crowded restaurant and agreed that game night may have been the reason. Everyone was trying to grab a bite before the game started. As they waited for their meals, Steve went back to his attempts at reassurance.

"I don't want you to think this is one-sided. I don't expect to lay back and have you do all the work. I really do," he reached across the table for her hand, "want to spend the night with you. Get to know you. You're intriguing to me. Have been since you came to the auction."

Imani blushed. She was so nervous. She hoped he couldn't feel her palm sweating into his.

"I've got a reputation to uphold, so I need to make sure you're just as satisfied as I am when you leave me. Gotta seal the deal for a repeat," he smiled his widest smile.

Imani couldn't catch herself. She burst out laughing at his humor and presumptuousness. She was put at ease by his lightheartedness about the situation. Jackie brought out her rib basket and his pulled pork sandwich. They both bowed their heads briefly before beginning to eat.

"Okay," Imani finally found the nerve, or maybe it was the degree of comfort, to address her concerns and curiosities.

"You're a handsome, intelligent, successful man. Why are you…" her voice trailed off, "willing to pay for my time and sex?"

Steve took a bite of his sandwich, chewed and swallowed. Wiping the excess barbecue sauce away with a napkin, he took a deep breath before responding.

"Look," he said, sternly, "I've tried my hand at love, and they're all after the money at the end of it all. My first wife took everything I had, which was ironic, because when I met her she had nothing. And," he wiped his mouth again with his napkin, "she wasn't worth a dime of it. She was beautiful to look at, but had a terribly nasty demeanor. She was lazy, couldn't cook, and after she knew she had me, laid like a log in the sack."

Imani shook her head. Some women take shit for granted, she thought.

He continued, "I ended up getting a maid and a cook, and an escort that I frequented. So in my mind, I feel like I should pay those who deserve it. Time is valuable. I'm sure you could be somewhere else, doing something else, but you chose to indulge me," he paused, looking directly into her eyes so she knew he meant the next statement. "So have no doubt, I intend to make sure it is worth your while, and not just financially. We are going to have a blast, both in and out of the bedroom."

Imani smiled with closed lips, hiding her mouth full of ribs. She chewed as Steve laughed at the face she must've been making. When she finally swallowed, she replied, "Sounds like a plan to me. But, I must ask," she took a sip of her Dr. Pepper, "how does the payment part work? And what are your sexual preferences?"

He smiled at her directness and her desire to get the particulars defined. "I'll give you half tonight and the other half before you leave on Sunday. You're not locked into spending every waking moment with me, unless you choose to. But I do ask that you join me for at least one meal a day from now until I check out on Sunday."

Imani lifted her hand to stop him, "Steve, for that kind of money, you have me with you all weekend."

He smiled and raised his glass of tea for a toast, "To an eventful weekend…"

Imani clinked her glass to his, "Cheers."

The rest of the meal was filled with the usual getting-to-know-you conversation. They bonded over their disdain for their exes and the mutual feeling that they were idiots for making such bad choices. When they finished their meal, they walked out of Dreamland grinning. They got swept into the mob of spectators, all headed down the street to Biscuit Stadium. Steve wrapped his arm around Imani's waist so that he wouldn't lose her. Imani willingly accepted the masculine gesture. The first of many that she would enjoy throughout the weekend. She had never once considered dating a white man. She was concerned with the stares and comments they would be badgered with in a city like Montgomery. She feared what their children may have to face growing up mixed, especially in a closed-minded, secretly segregated city like this one. On top of the fact that she thought white penises were ugly.

Imani looked around at some of the faces that were being made at them. This confirmed her concerns. But this weekend, Imani could care less about what anyone thought. She slipped her hand around his waist and enjoyed the affection. At Biscuit Stadium, Steve bought them beer and explained the game to her. They had plenty of time to talk because, as Imani soon learned, baseball was quite a slow game. Halfway through, they were hungry again.

Steve told her he loved being around the crowd, which is why he hadn't gotten seats in any of the boxes up high. He bought Imani a Polish sausage with onions and peppers and called it blasphemy when she put mayo on top of the relish, ketchup, and mustard. They ate boiled peanuts and he devoured nachos with cheese, jalapeños and bacon. By the third huge beer, neither of them cared who won. They stayed and watched the fireworks after the game. On their way out of the Stadium, Steve offered to give Imani a piggyback ride because she was in heels and a little under the influence. The last thing he needed was for her to twist her ankle. Imani rode his back all the way to the hotel. Steve seemed to hold his alcohol a bit better than her.

When they got into the parking lot of the Embassy Suites, she got down, stopped at her car to get her purse and overnight bag from the trunk, and walked the rest of the way with his arm around her waist to aid in her balance. When they got into the elevator, his hand slid down her back, over it's sway to her ass. Much to her own surprise, Imani didn't flinch or pull away. Steve felt a tension in his pants in excited anticipation of what was about to happen. She'd been as pleasant as he'd expected. A real fun girl. Blending in so well in surroundings that were obviously unfamiliar to her. She'd been responsive to his touch, even enjoying it. And he'd taken his time, swallowing his eagerness to move forward, to feeling every part of her. To give everyone in the Biscuit Stadium a real fireworks show.

Even now, he was practicing a great deal of restraint. Her ass was round and soft. He wanted to grab it with both hands, press her up against one wall of the elevator, feel the space in between the wood and her lower back where the arch wouldn't touch. Wanted to kiss her passionately.

Why the hell is this elevator taking so long? Steve wondered, his mind losing the blood flow tug-of-war to his dick. He was as excited as a virgin on prom night. But knowing this, he tried to calm himself because he didn't want to finish prematurely.

She didn't help. The look she gave him when the doors opened and they exited the elevator said yes to everything.

Let The Games Begin

I wanna give my all
To someone I love
But right now,
Money talks…

Steve walked Imani down the hallway with a firm grip on her ass. He didn't even let go when opening the door to the suite. She smiled to herself at the level of self-control he was showing. He continued to impress her when he allowed her to go freshen up, taking her overnight bag into the bathroom with her. Closing the door, she looked at her reflection. She took out Summer's Eve Feminine wipes and after relieving herself of what felt like all of the beer she'd drank, she patted herself dry with tissue, cleansed the sweat from her vagina with the wipes, and kicked her pants off. She took off her shirt, adjusted her breasts in her lace bra, changed into a pair of red patent leather, six-inch pumps, and sprayed a few squirts of Body by Victoria's Secret onto her skin.

She looked over her reflection one more time, gave herself a nervous grin, and walked towards the door. Opening the door, she found that Steve hadn't let the time pass him by. He'd lit candles along the dresser and on the nightstand. The speakers of a CD player were filling the room with Miles Davis and John Coltrane's In A Sentimental Mood. He sat, fully clothed, in the armchair across the room, beside the window. Imani walked towards him slowly. On her way across the room, she saw an array of toys on the footstool at the bottom of the bed. There were handcuffs, a blindfold, feather tickler, and what she hoped was just a massager because of the large, bulbous tip on it. She fought the curiosity of whether he'd gone shopping after she'd called and accepted his offer or if he traveled with a sex kit.

"They're new," Steve said, apparently following her glance. "Well, all but the massager. That's my secret weapon."

Imani blushed and continued her saunter towards him. She reached her destination and straddled him, finding a full, very impressive erection beneath her. She'd been concerned, based on her previous assumptions and reports from others who had been with white men, that she was gonna have to try out her acting chops. She'd expected him to be short and thick. Not enough to even get her near an orgasm which was why, she assumed, he'd bought all of those accessories.

She slow grinded in Steve's lap working her hips with her back arched, breasts pushed forward. She looked into his eyes, realizing for the first time that they were blue with specks of green in them. He was handsome. His brown hair had grey strands sprinkled through it. He had a strong jaw line, resemblant of Brad Pitt, a slim, not too pointy nose, and thin lips that housed a beautifully perfect set of straight, white teeth. She ran her hands through his hair and down his face, lifting his chin. She pressed her lips against his, parting them slightly, to invite his tongue. His hands moved from the arms of the chair to her hips before gripping her ass. She kept moving in his lap while the song changed to Kind of Blue. His hands massaged every inch of her as his tongue slid in and out her mouth in one of the sexiest rhythms Imani had ever experienced.

He stood up, lifting her up out of the chair. She wrapped her legs around his waist and her arms around his neck as he carried her to the bed. Laying her down, he kissed all of her that was uncovered, even slid her shoes off and sucked her toes. She moaned and giggled at the sensations. Feet were so sensitive and it was a rarity for a man to put his mouth on them. In one swift, rather experienced motion, he'd managed to reach down to the footstool and grab the handcuffs. She laughed to herself because this entire situation was going totally opposite from what she'd seen in her head.

Imani had prepared for a night of pleasing Steve until the sun rose. But it seemed he had plans for her that involved very little effort on her part. As afraid as she was to allow him to handcuff her, she let go of herself and let him get his money's worth. He laid the handcuffs on the nightstand to her right and picked up a bottle of massage oil. She also saw a box of Trojan Magnum condoms on the nightstand. Had she not felt his erection for herself, she would have scoffed at the thought of him fitting plus-sized condoms, thinking he was delusional. But she had no doubt they were absolutely the right size.

Imani lifted herself up on her elbows. She met eyes with the fully-clothed man standing over her, before sitting all the way up and taking the bottle of oil. She placed it back on the table, then grabbed his shirt at the bottom.

"We don't want to ruin your clothes, now do we?" Imani smiled coyly, sitting up on her knees.

She lifted his shirt over his head and flung it into the armchair. She sat back on her heels, taking full inventory of his toned upper body. His chest was clean shaven. There was a beautiful, tribal tattoo that covered his left pectoral muscle. There was no mistaking what it was. Medusa glared back at her, green tinted skin between the large, interlocking tribal lines, eyes red as fire, and hair spiraling unkempt from her head. It was breathtaking. Steve was getting to be more and more intriguing by the moment. His stomach was hard enough to scrub clothes on. Imani knew she was going to enjoy kissing every part of his body.

He stood and allowed her to take in his body, enjoying every moment of it and the way her face showed exactly what she was thinking. He even made his pecs jump a couple of times for her. His flirtation made her excitement rise and caused Imani to go back to work undressing him. She pulled at the larger than usual University of Alabama belt buckle, freeing his belt and unbuttoning his shorts. They fell to the floor as she unzipped them and she was met with yet another surprise. Nothing but bare skin remained as his Cyclops stared back at her. He was well above average length and width. More than Imani had felt when she was lap dancing. She giggled on the inside at the way that it hooked slightly to the left. She began to lean forward, her mouth seeming to gravitate towards his waist, eager to taste him. Steve stepped back a little, just enough to be out of her reach.

"In due time," he said.

He patted the bed. "I want you right here."

Imani laughed. "This is your show, huh?"

She conceded. Laying in the bed obediently on her stomach, just to the left of where he'd requested. This gesture sent the message that she was willing to do as told, but was still in control of this situation as much as he was. Steve's face lit up loving the way she challenged him, even if subtly. He nodded towards her as he reached for the massage oil again, letting her know that her message was read loud and clear.

He admired her body as he squeezed the cherry-flavored, warming massage oil into his palm. Rubbing his hands together, he tried to decide where to begin. Her shoulders, elongated neck, toned back, round behind, or those legs that seemed to go on for miles. Steve was going to have to tap into all of his will power to maintain his composure while rubbing her down. He chose to begin at her feet and work his way up. He saw her muscles tighten as he took her left foot into his hands. He massaged from soles to toes, putting pressure on her pleasure points. He focused on the ball of her foot, which was rough from constantly wearing heels. Imani moaned in response to his touch, squealing as he placed her toes into his mouth. Its warmth provided a pleasant compliment to the tingle of the massage oil. Steve repeated this with her right foot.

She was trying to hold herself together but giggles, moans and loud, throaty grunts betrayed her. Steve worked his way up the path of her legs with the oil, having to pause twice to re-oil his palms. They were long, longer than expected on a woman of five-foot-two inches. They were softly toned like those of a former athlete who still squatted, walked, or jogged occasionally. Her ass was confirmation of this. It was small, but soft and perfectly round. There was a cuff just above her thighs where the skin creased and laid at the top of her legs, making it perfectly grippable. Steve used both hands to indulge in it. Lifting and spreading the flesh of it, nibbling on each cheek before allowing his tongue to venture in between them. He loved how she responded. Her body tensed, relaxed, tensed again. She squealed. A higher-pitched squeal than before. Then moaned repeatedly as his tongue went in and out of her hole. He continued this until she locked up and shrieked in orgasm.

He'd wanted this woman for so long. Now that he had her, and for an entire weekend. He was going to indulge his every fantasy of her, every thought he'd had while watching her at the auction. She truly had no idea what he had in store for her.

Steve continued up to her back. Loving the way it dipped from the top of her ass. That bend was going to be sexy to watch from behind. Ah, the things I'm going to do to this woman, he thought.

Steve worked up her back, putting more pressure on these muscles. His erection was full and hard, beginning to hurt as he enjoyed the feel of her body under his hands. He maintained focus. Worked out all pressure from her neck and shoulders. He grabbed the burning candle from the nightstand and dripped hot wax onto her back. His dick jumped as she screamed when the wax hit her flesh. She convulsed again, indicating orgasm. Steve knew she was ready and willing to go as far as he would take her.

His mind was flooded with vivid images. Pushing them away quickly, as not to make his overexcitement any worse, he knew he would have plenty of time to make those thoughts into reality. He must have paused, engulfed in his thoughts, long enough for Imani to notice. She took the opportunity to pounce. She turned around quickly wrapping her warm, wet mouth around his erection, taking him in until her face met his pelvis. This caught Steve completely off-guard and, combined with the feeling of her mouth, made him lose his composure, cumming almost immediately.

His cheeks flushed red in embarrassment. Imani didn't notice. She was too busy massaging the rest of the cum from him and getting him back up to full erection. Back up in a matter of seconds, Steve didn't waste another moment. He tore open a Magnum wrapper and stepped back, far enough for his body to be out of range of her mouth. He unrolled the latex onto his skin. Imani removed her bra and thong. She laid back on the bed, on her back, legs spread, welcoming him into her. He was overcome with excitement as he got into the bed and on top of this beautiful woman. She was wet. Dripping wet. But he didn't enter her immediately. He kissed her. Passionately. Letting their tongues dance and their hands travel all over one another's bodies.

He loved the way her small breasts fit into his large palms. He couldn't wait to put them in his mouth. The way her back arched when she laid on her back in the bed. Her small frame fit beneath him with room to spare. It made him feel manly. He trailed kisses down her neck, cuffing her breast in his hand before taking her large, dark brown nipple into his mouth. She responded unexpectedly, squealing and squirming. He'd apparently found her spot. This encouraged Steve to play with them. Licking them, one at a time. Sucking until they stood erect. Hershey's kisses on her chest.

She kicked and shifted her weight beneath him, trying unsuccessfully to get away from his mouth. He loved her inability to control herself, especially knowing her desire to maintain control. He kept at it, sliding her back into place every time she wiggled away. When she climaxed, orgasming all over the bed, he grabbed his erection. He rubbed it up and down against her clit, prolonging her orgasm before sliding his head into her pulsating opening. He knew his girth, which made him take his time working himself into her. To his surprise, she wrapped her legs around his back and pulled him on into her with a deep, throaty sigh.

She took him, all of him, fitting perfectly. He hit her bottom, felt her walls. He couldn't remember the last time a woman felt as good as she did to him. He almost lost his composure again. He was well on the way to embarrassing himself for a second time. She was more divine than he could've imagined. He couldn't have her thinking that he'd done all that work with the foreplay just to lead to the anti-climactic repetition of a premature nut. He had to use an old trick he hadn't used since high school.

Z, y, x, w, v, u… he recited the alphabet backwards until she began to shake beneath him. He couldn't look at her because her face, the way she bit her lip, squinted her eyes and crinkled her nose, would make him lose his focus. He planned to bend her over after this. But then, he doubted this woman was unappealing at any angle, and he knew maintaining composure would be twice as hard because he would go deeper from behind.

The way she knew her body, the way she moved it, controlling his stroke with her legs, guiding him in and out, was so sexy. She would shift her hips slightly to heighten her own pleasure. Steve found himself getting excited again, ready to burst. She started to roll her hips, her pelvis slightly off the bed. The rhythm of their sex caused the headboard to bang on the wall behind it. Boomp. Boomp. Boomp. Boo-boomp. Boo-boomp. And her moans, loud and intense, were the melody to the beat. They danced. Doing the horizontal tango. It was something almost spiritual about the way everything moved and meshed in unison, two becoming one. Normally, women squirmed beneath him. They couldn't take all of him, complaining about him being too big. Most of them surpassed Imani by inches in height and tens of pounds in weight. Steve was baffled by it, but loving it so much he was unable to maintain.

He felt her legs tighten around his waist, pulling him all the way into her. The walls tightened around his dick and a stream of warm, wet fluid hit his pelvis and streamed down his thighs. He paused but her face said to go on. He pulled out and pushed back inside of her. More liquid. Over and over. The sensation was something he'd never felt before. This was some porn star shit. Making a woman squirt was as mythical to most men as a unicorn. Steve was like a kid in a candy store.

He'd completely forgotten about his impending nut. Making Imani make that sexy ass face, a cross between extreme pleasure and pain with just a hint of embarrassment, was fine. She'd glued herself up against the headboard. She couldn't run any further and those big, almond shaped eyes were opened as wide as they could go. She was biting her bottom lip. The screaming had ceased, the CD had run out of tracks, and all that filled the silence now was the headboard providing the beat to the glorious sound of their bodies squishing together, now both soaked in Imani's pleasure from the waist down.

Now how do I ask room service to come change the sheets this time of night and without embarrassing Imani? he wondered to himself. He would figure that out later. Right now, he was enjoying the mess being made. He didn't switch his position, just moved in and out of her. He didn't want to lose the sweet spot. He'd found a magic button and was in the process of making mental notes of everything. He wanted to be able to repeat this as often as he could. He was focused so hard on his mental documentation, he didn't realize until it was too late, that she'd started massaging his sack and tightening her walls simultaneously. One more squeeze from her and he came himself.

Damn, this woman was good, he thought, as he rolled over beside her on the bed.

Both of them laid in a puddle of sweat and other juices. They both struggled to catch their breath. Steve smiled as his chest heaved. This was definitely money well spent. Now to call for maid service.

Anywhere

I can love you in the shower
Both of our bodies drippin' wet
On the patio
We can make a night you won't forget…

Imani rolled toward Steve and kissed him on the shoulder. She sat up and scooted out of the bed, walking across the room towards the bathroom. Steve smiled at the endearing gesture. He rolled over across the wetness she'd left all over the bed and picked up the phone from its cradle. He requested maid service, new sheets, chocolate covered strawberries and champagne before getting up to blow out the dwindling candles and join Imani in the shower. When he walked into the bathroom, steam filled the space, along with the scent of her Pomegranate body wash.

He pulled back the cloth curtain and found her lathered in suds, bending over to wash her feet. Her tattooed brown skin was cloaked in white suds and bent over so that her booty was fully rounded. It was inviting and made him stand at attention. She must've felt his eyes on her, or maybe it was the draft from the curtain being open and all the steam exiting into the stall, because she stopped and looked back at him with a sexy smile and a wink.

Steve smiled back, getting into the shower with her. She turned around to face him, squeezing soap onto the washcloth and bathing him from head to toe. It was one of the sexiest things Steve had ever had done to him. She was so slow and thoughtfully methodical with her movements. She catered to his body, paying special attention to each of his fingers, his erect penis, even his toes. He stood there in complete awe and admiration of the act she was performing as if it were normal to bathe a man. When she finished, she stepped to the side to allow the hot water to rinse him clean and when Steve stepped forward, Imani exited the shower.

By the time Steve was done rinsing himself, Imani had dried her body and was applying lotion. He turned the water off and stepped out onto the cold tile floor. He dried himself as she finished lotioning up and went to the sink to brush her teeth. She wrapped one towel around her body and another in an upward style around her hair. She looked so regal. She caught his reflection watching her as she looked up from spitting and laughed aloud. A deep laugh that rumbled through the room. One that fit her broad, perfect-toothed, ear-to-ear smile. And it was contagious. Steve found himself laughing right along with her. He walked up behind her, wrapped his arms around her waist and took in their reflection in the glass. She laid her head back into his chest, as if instinctually, and flashed another broad smile at their appearance.

He turned her around to face him and kissed her. He grabbed her under her ass, picked her up off her feet, and sat her on the vanity. He pushed the towel back from her thighs and made a beeline to her lap. With his lips, he pushed the hood of her clit back and alternated between sucking on it and stroking it with his tongue in an up and down motion. Imani squealed her enjoyment of the oral gratification, her body jerking. Steve went from this to tongue fucking her. He felt her start throbbing against his chin. He loved the way her muscles constricted. She could make them tight enough to bear hug anything that was in her, be it tongue, finger, or phallus. He enjoyed the sensation. The warmth of her insides, mixed with the pressure from her walls, was erotic.

After several orgasms, he untied the knot at her breasts and the towel fell back onto the vanity. He kissed her, his face wet with her orgasm. She wrapped her arms around his neck and her legs around his waist, pulling him as close to her as their separate bodies would allow. Steve had his right hand on the back of her neck and, with his left, he directed himself to her opening. He slid into her wetness. She directed his stroke with her legs, slow and deep. Bit his bottom lip when he would hit her bottom. As it started to get good to her, she leaned back, pressing her head and shoulders against the mirror. They both sighed heavily. Steve leaned forward into Imani, steadying himself against the mirror with his right hand. With his left, he lifted her right leg up onto his shoulder, opening her up to him even more.

Her sighs turn to screams as he dug deeper into her. She called his name and God's between curses as she neared orgasm. Steve buried face into her neck, the nutty smell of her shea butter cream filling his nose, making her smell edible. He nibbled her earlobes. Sucked and licked the length of her neck. The towel that was on her head fell into the sink but neither of them missed a beat. She felt even better without the rubber between them.

Her flesh was hot and moist and Steve was able to feel every bit of her. He put her other leg onto his right shoulder, using the vanity as a brace. Both hands gripping the small of her back, he leaned into her body even more, folding her nearly in half at the waist. Her toes were pressed against the mirror's glass. Her screams got louder. So loud it felt they were shaking the walls. And…

One long, loud, screeching howl later, liquid squirted onto his stomach, the vanity, and began trickling down to the floor. Steve kept going. He'd gotten his second wind and wanted to give her as much pleasure as his body would allow. He drilled her, fast and hard, until she was hoarse from the screaming and there was a puddle of her pleasure at his feet. Her body slid around on the vanity from the fluids.

Taking things to the next level, Steve grabbed Imani around the neck, squeezing slightly. Her whole body tensed up as she closed her eyes tight, enjoying the new sensation. Steve, excited once again by her openness, pushed in one more powerful, deep time, and then pulled out quickly, ejaculating all over the flaming lotus tattoo on her stomach. Her legs fell limp onto the vanity, dangling on either side of his body.

Taking the corner of the abandoned towel, he used to dry portion to wipe the semen off her. He picked her up and carried her out of the bathroom. She wrapped her arms around his back and enjoyed the chivalry. Opening the door, he realized they had been so engulfed in the act that they hadn't heard the maid come in and change the sheets or set the wine and chocolate covered strawberries on the nightstand.

The room, dimly lit by the soft glow of the nightstand lamp, was comforting. Steve laid Imani down, gently on the clean, dry bed. While he opened the wine and filled their glasses, Imani fumbled in the nightstand drawer, pushing the phone book and the Bible to the side, in search of the remote. She pulled it out and propped herself up against the pillows and the headboard. She turned the television to TNT for their Law & Order marathon. Scooting over, she patted the bed for Steve to join her. He placed the tray of chocolate covered strawberries between them on the bed and they sipped the wine and fed one another the dessert between discussions of the plot of each episode. Imani revealed her desire to be an attorney when she was younger. This, of course was after her dreams of becoming a stripper, veterinarian and a journalist, all of which her mother shot down.

He told her about the wine they were drinking, Miss Scarlett, a sweet Alabama red wine from the Vinizini's Wine Farm in Calera,

Alabama. They laughed and cuddled once the sweets were gone. After her second glass of wine, Imani's speech began to slur. She nestled her body against his, resting her head on his chest and slid into a calm sleep. He watched her rest. Sometimes, her breathing would accelerate, becoming very labored, and her body would flinch. He wondered what plagued her dreams. After an episode and a half more of Law & Order, Steve felt his eyes getting heavy. He pulled Imani close to him, took a deep breath of her soft, fluffy hair and slipped into his own unconsciousness.

Laughing All The Way To The Bank

I hop up out the bed,
Get my swag on...
I look in the mirror say what's up
What's up. What's up. What's up.

The sun filled the room, waking Imani with its light. She shifted around the bed, finding that she had it all to herself. The room was quiet. The TV had been turned off, the toys were put up, and there was an empty tray, two wine glasses, and a bottle of Miss Scarlett, with more than half of its contents gone on the nightstand. There was a fluffy white envelope with her name written neatly in small black letters on the front.

She picked the envelope up and pulled out the hand written note, on hotel stationery, that was wrapped around a ridiculous amount of money. At least it was ridiculous in Imani's mind. Even at only half of what Steve was going to pay her, she had enough money to pay her debt and use the money from the pawn shop as a nest egg. She thought about just taking what she had and calling an end to the situation. She wrestled with this in her mind as she read his note:

Imani,

I am a man of my word, so here is the first half of the amount we'd agreed upon. Truth be told, just your company was worth this much and more. I had to run home because there was some urgent business that required my hands-on attention. I will be back Saturday evening and would love to see more of you. The room is paid for and I left you the spare key card in this envelope. The hospitality desk has also been informed that you are my guest. Kick back and enjoy yourself, order some room service. Consider it a mini-staycation. On me. (Smile)

Hope to see you soon,

Steve

Imani smiled as, once again, Steve had made her an offer she couldn't refuse. He had been nothing but kind to her so this weekend was far nicer, thus far, than anything she could have imagined. She was curious to see how the rest of it would go when he returned. She laid out the bills and counted them. All hundreds. Twenty-five total. The key card fell out of the now empty envelope into her lap. She decided she would go to the bank... Later.

She placed the note, money and key card back into the envelope, tucked it under her pillow, and turned the TV on. She watched more of the Law & Order marathon she'd fallen asleep on the night before. Soon she began to doze off again. She could rest better knowing her financial troubles had been resolved. And after this weekend, she would never give Keith the room to place her in such a compromising position again. As a matter of fact, his name would be listed on the list of those who did not have permission to check Zion out or even visit her at her new school. Since he'd given her full legal and physical custody, she was sure making this happen wouldn't be difficult.

Imani felt a calm come over her as she fell asleep. Her worries melted into the pillow. When she woke again, it was late afternoon. She decided to get up, make her deposit, talk to Zion, check her apartment to make sure that it hadn't been broken into in her absence, and grab something to eat. She went into the bathroom to take a wash-up and get dressed. She laughed at the mess they'd made of the vanity. She laughed even harder as she thought of the conversation she was sure the staff was having about them. From the soaked sheets to the toys on the footstool, and she knew the maids heard them in the bathroom last night, they had plenty to talk about. Hell, Imani wouldn't be surprised that the entire floor heard them, or at least heard her. She blushed. She was definitely going to get some stares for the rest of the weekend, so she decided she might as well go all out.

I've got some plans for Steve Reynolds, she smiled as she shimmied into her denim booty shorts and pulled her Eye of Ra off-the-shoulder tee over her head. She put on her big door knocker earrings, not even bothering to clean up the mess, and just reached around it to wash her face, brush her teeth, and pick her hair. She sat on the commode and put on her black patent leather pumps and packed her overnight bag.

Walking out of the bathroom, she tossed the bag onto the footstool, reached beneath the pillow to get her envelope, and put it in her purse. She took one last look, laughing at the room again, before closing the door. She rode the elevator down to the lobby and smiled at the stares she got from employees and guests alike. She went to the Hospitality Desk and told them that room 412 needed maid service. Danny, the Guest Services Rep that she spoke with, gave her a double take. He'd apparently made the connection that she was the white gentleman's guest.

He smiled and gave her a wink. "Yes, ma'am," he replied. Smothering a chuckle.

"Thank you!" Imani laughed for the both of them. She turned on her heels and walked towards the doors. She had to fight the urge to skip to her car in excitement as she hurried to get to the bank and deposit the money in her purse before it mysteriously disappeared, or she woke up and realized that this was all a dream.

At the drive-through at Alabama State Employees Credit Union on Washington Avenue, Imani filled out her deposit slip as she waited her turn in line. It must've been payday because the line was long. Usually, this would've annoyed her and she would've pulled off and tried her luck at the Perry Hill Road branch or the Service Center on Atlanta highway. But today, she sat patiently as the line eased along.

She'd removed her Driver's License and the money from the Pawn Shop from her wallet, less the remaining $75 from the hundred she'd broken at Applebee's. She was going to put $2000 in her savings and the rest in checking so that she could get a money order for that incompetent ass daycare director. The rest would be used to register Zion in Calvary Christian Academy. She'd been told that she wouldn't have to make her first payment for 30 days, but she planned to pay that too, to give herself a head start. The child support that Keith was ordered to pay was enough to pay Imani's rent and utilities, so she could use her paycheck from her new job to cover the cost of Zi's tuition. Her paycheck from the Auction would pick up the slack in the months that Keith didn't pay like he was supposed to. She'd try her best not to touch what was in savings.

Imani was playing out scenarios in her head as the line moved forward, one car at a time. She was so excited about having a financial cushion that she didn't even get annoyed with the woman in front of her who broke the rule posted several times before reaching the teller, limiting each vehicle to two transactions. She could've sworn she saw the woman sent and receive the tube a good twelve times. Imani laughed as the cars in the lane beside hers started and finished their business and went on about their lives. After the fourth one pulled off, the one in front of her moved on.

The exasperated look on the teller, Michelle's, face was priceless. Imani imagined she was a pretty girl minus the scowl. She greeted

Imani as best as she could through her frustration. Imani was very familiar with the frustrations that accompany customer service work. She smiled her biggest smile and didn't take the woman's demeanor personally. She even cracked a few jokes to cheer her up. By the end of the encounter, Imani had fixed the teller's face.

She pulled forward so the next customer could be served. She paused at the stop sign at the end of the Credit Union parking lot and looked at the receipt. She smiled to herself and then looked at the gas gauge to see how much she'd used. She'd get gas after she checked on her house. She traveled the few streets up from the Credit Union to her home. She turned into the parking lot of her apartment complex and parked right in front of her loft. She was heavy in her thoughts as she walked up the walkway to her home. Everything looked pretty normal. Everything was in the place where she left it. Relieved that her meager belongings were intact, she called her mom and told her she was coming to spend time with Zion and that they needed to talk. She double-checked her doors and windows, knowing she would be gone for another two nights. She wasn't going to make a break-in easy for anyone.

Imani headed through Downtown to her mother's house in the Buckingham Neighborhood. As she drove towards the Southside of town, she became saddened by the way the scenery changed. Buildings with clean windows, full parking lots, and beautiful landscapes became empty buildings with boarded up windows, parking lots full of inoperable cars, and high grass and dying trees. The upkeep of the Southside was not a major concern of the City of Montgomery, but it sure was a popular hangout for the police. Roadblocks and speed traps littered the entire area, but it still took half an hour to get a police officer to show up when 911 was called.

Imani thought of the hotel she'd just left with a man who could afford to spend $5000 for weekend with a stranger. Then, she looked around again, as she sat at the traffic light at Narrow Lane Road and Southern Boulevard. Her reality was recognized. She was living in a part of town where she had to check on her house when she was gone overnight to make sure it had not been broken into. She was a woman accepting money for sex from a white man, a stranger, to get herself out of a financial bind. A man she'd met at her job. She'd allowed him inside of her without a rubber and even though he pulled out, there were bigger things to be concerned with than pregnancy. Especially since he'd admitted that he partook in the exchange of sexual acts for money pretty regularly.

Imani began to second-guess her decisions, especially with this situation. What happens if word gets out about this? I could lose my job. I could find out in two weeks that I've contracted something. Word could get out that I had sex for money. As a mother, all of these scenarios kept playing on her conscience.

She pulled into the Pace Car gas station on the corner of Narrow Lane Road and the Southern Boulevard. She walked in and greeted the cashier, "As-Salaam-Alaikum."

This threw him completely off-guard. He watched her, dressed in a non-Muslim manner, walking down the candy aisle. She picked up Green Apple Sour Punch Straws, Boston Baked Beans, and two bottles of Smart Water from the cooler. When she placed her merchandise on the counter, the cashier furrowed his brow at her a bit. Still confused.

"Is that all for you today?" he asked in his thick Arab accent.

"No sir," Imani responded with a grin. "May I please have thirty on pump number four also?"

The cashier rang up the gas. "Your total is $38.42," he informed Imani, never taking his eyes off of her face.

Imani counted out the amount in exact change. Before she walked away, she answered the question that was written all over his face. "No, sir. I'm not Muslim. I just have a great deal of respect for your beliefs."

The cashier's face relaxed and he flashed a smile. "Wa alaikum assalam," he replied proudly as Imani pushed open the door and exited the building.

She walked to her pump and pulled it from its holster. Choosing her gas, she ignored the men who stood watching her put the nozzle in the gas tank. She stared at the digital numbers as they counted up the number of gallons and the dollar amount. She laughed as she thought about the amount gas was per gallon when she started driving. A mark of age, she thought to herself.

She finished her pump and reset the nozzle. She got into her car and pulled off onto Narrow Lane Road towards her mother's house. As she got closer, she realized that she may have wanted to think twice about her outfit. She knew how her mother was and had been having too good of a day to deal with that shit today.

Oh well, Imani thought to herself as she took the right turn onto Sunshine Drive, I already know what's coming so I might as well get my mind ready. Imani paused longer than necessary at the four-way stop sign. She took the time to pull a Filter Tip Black & Mild from her cigarette case and remove the wrapper. The red Dodge that had pulled up behind her honked their frustration at her holding up their progress. Imani decided to take the long way to her mom's house and pulled off, passing her turn and continuing on Sunshine Drive. She pushed her car's cigarette lighter and, as she continued winding through the neighborhood she grew up in, waited for it to heat up and pop out.

As she continued on Sunshine towards Buckingham Drive, the lighter popped out loudly, abruptly, and she pulled it out, lit the tip of the Black & Mild, and cracked the window so the smoke flowed out. She took hard pulls the more she thought about her mother and the remarks that were sure to come from her mouth.

Imani smoked all the way through the neighborhood, from Sunshine to Buckingham and onto Norman Bridge Road. She looped back around, heading east on Southern Boulevard and turning back onto Narrow Lane Road. By the time she had passed the Pace Car service station, her Black was done and she prepared her mind for the inevitable.

She laughed to herself as she realized that, in the time it had taken her drive through the neighborhood, she could've gone home and changed. She settled on the fact that she was tired of making changes to appease her mother and turned back into the neighborhood. She took the right route to the house on Coventry Road that she grew up in.

When she pulled up, Zion, who was helping her Nana in the garden, dropped her mini shovel and ran to the edge of the driveway.

"Mommy!" she yelled enthusiastically, throwing her little arms around her mom's bare legs and pressing her face into her mother's thighs.

"Hey, baby," Imani laughed at her little girl's excitement to see her. She bent down and picked Zion up.

She was getting to be a big girl, but Imani could still hoist her comfortably up on her right hip. She kicked off her pumps to maintain balance, and walked across the concrete. Stepping onto the soft, cool grass she walked towards the stone garden in her mom's spacious front yard. Zion enjoyed bouncing on her mother's hip as she walked and played in her hair and with her earrings.

Cheryl, Imani's mom, looked up from her gardening and gave her daughter a once over. She wrinkled up her nose and Imani braced herself what was coming next.

"Girl, where the rest your clothes? You walkin' around here half-naked," she frowned at her child, her disapproval apparent on her face.

Imani sighed, "I have on clothes, Mama."

She knew that argument was useless. But she wasn't going to take her mother's shit sitting down today.

"Child," her mother sucked her teeth, "you walkin' around here like you sixteen years old. You're somebody's mama. Embarrassing your child like that…"

"Momma," Imani cut her off mid-tangent, "Zion doesn't seem too embarrassed to me. As a matter of fact," she bounced her big girl on her hip, pausing to kiss her on the cheek, "she doesn't seem to give a damn about what I'm wearing."

Cheryl said no more. She stood up, dusted the dirt off her hands before removing her gloves, and extending her arms for a hug, a sign of a truce. Imani wrapped her free arm around her mother. In her sixties, Cheryl looked every bit of thirty years old. She stood five-feet-two-inches tall, pleasantly thick, with a body that would make women Imani's age ashamed. She had big eyes, with tiny moles sprinkled underneath and across the tops of her cheeks. She had beautiful, full lips and a round face. Her hair was dark gray and texturized, making it curly. Normally, she covered it with wigs but on days like today, she wore it pulled into a ponytail, and you could see the baldness on her temples that physicians said was caused by bad nerves.

"Come on in the house before you cause a damn accident," she slid another slick comment in as she led her daughter and granddaughter towards the door.

Imani let that one slide, following her mother into her childhood home. She stopped as she stepped on the pavement to pick up her shoes. She opened the screen door and placed Zion's feet on the cold, tile floor. Zion took off towards the spare room to play. Imani took this opportunity to tell her mother that she would be enrolling Zion in Calvary in a couple of weeks. She avoided the details of Keith not paying the daycare.

Her mother was so excited about the news that she was barely listening to Imani speak, anyway. She started rambling on about helping her pay tuition and aftercare, buying the uniforms and supplies Zion would need for school. Imani could barely get a word in edgewise, but she didn't mind it. She'd rather deal with this excitement than have her mother do what she does best, criticize every aspect of Imani's life, from her outfit to her job to what she needs to be doing with herself and for Zion. Imani rarely saw her mom smile in her direction when she didn't have Zion her arms. It was a nice feeling. Almost made what Imani was doing for the money acceptable.

"You got enough to pay for tuition?" Cheryl asked.

"I've got a little bit saved up," Imani told half a lie. Her mother didn't know that her savings balance took a glorious jump this morning and would take another after forty-eight more hours with Steve.

"Well good," her mother gave her half a smile.

She and Imani went on to plan pickups and drop-offs. Zion ran back and forth between her room at her Nana's and the kitchen. Finally, she grabbed Imani's hand and led her down the hallway for a makeover. As Zion played in her mother's hair and they polished one another's toes, she and Imani had an in-depth discussion about going to a new school.

"Good." Zion told her mother, "I'm happy to be going somewhere else. There's this girl Tyesha, who is always pulling my hair and tried to push me off the slide."

Imani had been in the midst of text to Nia about meeting her for pedicure when Zion shared this with her. She stopped mid-text and laid her phone on the bed beside her.

"Zi baby, why didn't you tell me about this little girl being mean to you?"

"Because I got her back, mommy," Zion explained, "the last time she pushed me, I pushed her back and she fell and ran to tell the teacher. They told Nana because she came and got me."

Imani snickered and picked up the phone to press send. "That's my girl," she said, laughing and putting her phone down to grab her daughter's beautiful round face with both hands. "I'm very proud of you."

Imani got up and walked over to the TV. She put the movie The Aristocats in and pressed play.

"Watch some TV, Zion. I'm gonna go and talk to your Nana some more. Then I got to go meet Auntie Nia and have to work this weekend," Imani paused slightly at the euphemizing of her activities for the rest of the weekend. She was gonna be working all right, "so you're going to be with Nana and Auntie this weekend, okay?"

"Okay," Zion smiled her acceptance, which made Imani feel kind of bad because her child was so accepting of the situation.

"I'll come say goodbye before I go," Imani promised.

"Yes ma'am," Zion responded between chuckles at scenes on the television screen.

Imani walked to the door. She turned around and looked at her baby who was growing up so fast. She was sitting amongst her teddy bears, the queen-sized bed almost swallowing her tiny body up. She had her legs crossed at the ankles and was completely engrossed in the animation flashing on the screen. Imani walked back into the kitchen where her mother was making hot dogs and French fries for Zi. She felt her phone vibrate letting her know that Nia was headed to Angel Nails on Carter Hill Road.

"So," Imani led into the conversation, "were you going to tell me about Zi's altercation at daycare?"

"If there was something to tell, I would have," Cheryl responded, her attention remaining on the food she was preparing.

"Okay," Imani paused, trying to control her growing frustration.

"Zion handled the little girl who'd been bullying her just like we taught her to. I handled the little heiffer's mother and that damn daycare director. What's her name again?"

"Ms. Johnson," Imani responded.

"Yeah. Her," Cheryl laughed, to herself. "That one there is dumb as a box of damned rocks. I was going to talk to you again today about putting Zi in Calvary, but you'd already made that decision."

"Momma, that lady pissed me off so bad the other day I wanted to scream!" Imani shared without delving into too much detail. "Thank you for handling the situation because I probably would have lost it," Imani huffed.

"I'm happy to help anyway I can, Imani. That's what family does. Let's get my baby out of that ghetto ass daycare and into a real school, where she can learn something other than how to Whip and Nae Nae. Most of them damn kids can't read and spell their names, but they can Dab, though."

Imani laughed as her phone rang. It was Nia. She answered it and gave her friend a quick promise that she was on her way to the nail shop. Imani hung up the phone and kissed her mother's hair.

"Thanks again, Ma," she said quickly before run-walking through the house to give her baby girl some loving and say her goodbye, as promised.

"Zi baby!" Imani burst into the room just as Everybody Wants to Be A Cat went off.

"Ma'am!" Zion almost jumped out of her skin.

"Oh, I didn't mean to scare you, honey," Imani apologized. "I just came to get some kisses and say bye."

"Okay," Zion stood up in the bed and began to run towards her mother, springing in the air.

Imani caught her, spun around one good time, hugging and kissing her repeatedly. "I love you. I love you. I love you," Imani sang.

"I love you, tooooooo," Zion sang back.

Imani laid her baby back on the bed. Kissing each dimple in her plump cheeks. "See you a couple of days, okay?"

"Yes, ma'am," Zion responded.

"I love you. I miss you. And I zrrbtt you," Imani said, giving her baby a raspberry on her juicy cheeks.

"I zrrbtt you right back," Zion said, returning the raspberry.

Cheryl came in with a tray of hot dogs and fries. "Who's hungry?" she asked.

"Meeee!" Zion replied excitedly. "Thank you, Nana," she said, placing the tray in her tiny lap.

"See you later, Mama," Imani said to her mother on the way out of the bedroom.

"Don't work too hard!" Her mother yelled down the hallway at her daughter, "Zi and I will try not to have too much fun."

The guilt struck a nerve with Imani as she left her mother's house, locking the door behind her. Having to work and not being able to spend as much time with Zion as she did when she was a housewife was killing her. And now, having sex to get out of the debt that Keith had gotten her into with the daycare was more than she could bear.

As she cranked up her car, she debated telling Nia what she'd gotten herself involved in. Though she knew her friend wouldn't judge, she was slightly embarrassed by her choice to sell her body to resolve the problem. She lit a Black and turned up the radio. Fantasia's Baby Mama was playing, ironically enough. Imani made the decision to tell her friend what she was into. She needed to get that shit off her chest.

That's What Friends Are For

For good times and bad times
I'll be by your side forever more.
That's what friends are for…

Imani whipped into the parking lot of the shopping center. She parked next to Nia's car and saw that her friend had been sitting there waiting on her. When she waved, Nia didn't respond. It took Imani a second to realize that she was on the phone. A few seconds more before she saw that her friend was in the midst of an argument. Imani got out her car and tapped on the passenger side window. Nia pressed the button to unlock the door. Imani got in quietly and listened to one side of the conversation.

"Are you fucking kidding me, Charles?" Nia yelled into the phone. "How the hell do you expect me to feel about this shit? We can barely afford the children we have and you tell me that you've gone and made another one! Is this what you do when you go to your boy's house? And you're so reckless with your dick that you didn't even care to put on a damn condom!"

She got quiet as a loud male voice boomed through the phone speaker.

"Don't you even try to justify this with what I did," Nia said, interrupting him and rubbing her growing belly. "You had two damn outside children in the six years we've been together. I've got at least one more before I'm in the same race with you."

Nia's frustration was all over her face.

Imani placed her hand reassuringly on her friend's shoulder. Nia looked up with eyes full of tears. Her sadness pissed Imani off. She'd watched for years in silence as Nia took Charles back after each separation and new child. Both friends had been a shoulder for one another to cry on over the years. Nia had been Imani's sanity through Keith's abuse and one of the few to support her and her decision to leave. On the same token, Imani had lost count of the number of times she'd had to console Nia after a phone call, or confrontation, or new pregnancy. Charles was a whore, but her friend loved him. She always accepted his children, when the mothers were mature enough to allow her to. She'd been pregnant at the same time as last girl and now she was pregnant again. It almost seemed like déjà vu.

"I'll be a whore! I'm just taking a page out of the book you've been writing for damn near decade!"

Imani was snapped out of her thoughts by her friend screaming emphatically into the phone and pressing the end button.

"It's never as dramatic hanging up a cell phone as when we used to slam the house phone into its cradle, huh, Nia?" Imani joked, making her friend laugh.

Nia laid her face, wet with tears, on her friend's shoulder. Imani grabbed Nia's hand and then extended her free hand. As was the ritual, Nia handed over her cell phone. Imani held the power button down until the phone powered off. She took her phone out of her purse and did the same. She put them both in her bag and kissed her friend's hair. She consoled her while she cried her heart out for the millionth time.

As angry as the situation made Imani, she knew voicing her opinion was not the best idea. That wasn't how their friendship was set up. Sounding boards and shoulders to cry on was what they offered each other in times like these. So Imani bit her tongue and just reminded her friend to breathe.

Why do we stop breathing when we cry? She wondered to herself. She didn't ponder this for too long because Nia's loud sobs vibrated through her. Her shoulder was wet from the tears falling from her friend's eyes.

Imani knew part of it was hormones but the majority of it was pain. So much pain. It filled the car. All of the lies, the cheating, the outside children poured from Nia's eyes, nostrils, and mouth. Imani stroked her hair, soothing her friend in complete silence. But internally, she was fuming. Nia cried for at least twenty minutes before finally calming down. She'd had to open her car door to vomit onto the pavement of the parking lot twice. When she looked at Imani, her eyes looked like she'd lost a fight with Pretty Boy Floyd.

Imani stifled a snicker at the sight of her friend's puffy face. The mascara ran in streaks down her cheeks. She looked so sad and pitiful. In her second trimester of pregnancy, Nia's already large breasts were even larger and her nose was beginning to spread. She had a cute little belly poking out in front of her and was starting to need to adjust her seat and struggled a little bit to get out of the car. Imani didn't envy her.

Nia was a breeder. She was all about family and wanted a big one. She was really old school. The cooking, cleaning, stand-by-her-man-even-if-he-fucks-up kind of woman. And Charles was a Grade A Fuck-up. Imani shook her head once again at the thought. Then another one crossed her mind. As she and Nia locked their doors and walked across the parking lot to the salon, Imani started doing the math.

Is it possible that it isn't Charles's baby Nia is pregnant with? She counted the months since their Girl's Night Out at The Mission House. Could it be? She wanted to know but chose not to ask because she didn't want to upset Nia anymore.

They signed their names to the list, chose their nail polish and waited silently, hand-in-hand, to be called. Imani stroked the back of Nia's hand with her thumb. Nia kept her eyes fixed on the floor. The thoughts that were running through her head flashed over her face one at a time. Her face was a movie screen for her pain.

Nia's head jerked up as their names were called. They walked together and were seated in soft, leather massage chairs. Imani ordered a glass of Cabernet and Nia a glass of Pinot Grigio. They sipped their wine and enjoyed the kneading of the massage chair on their backs and the women chatting jovially in Mandarin while rubbing their legs and working on their stiletto-calloused feet. Imani took this opportunity to tell Nia about Steve and her situation.

"So... Keith hasn't been paying Zi's daycare. It's so far past due there's no way I'm gonna be able to make it in the next week to keep her there."

"Girl, no! That nigga ain't gone let you rest 'til you're dead and he'll probably come dig you up then just to flip you over."

Imani laughed at how true that was. "Girl, you said somethin' then."

"So you need me to help you pay it?"

"Nope, I pawned my wedding set from Keith for some of it and the rest... well, let's just say it's been taken care of," Imani smirked.

"Uh oh. What the hell have you gotten yourself into?" Nia eyed her, suspiciously.

"Ummm... well, one of the dealers from the auction offered me money to spend the weekend with him."

Nia laughed in disbelief.

"Imani, I swear you find yourself in the craziest situations!" Nia laughed again, loud and bellowed.

"I know, Nia," Imani sighed sheepishly, "but I had to do something."

"You did something when you pawned your bridal set, Imani," her friend responded. "You didn't have to go to these extra lengths."

Imani knew her friend was offering more reason than judgment. Nia already knew Imani was too proud to ask for, or accept, hand-outs. She already felt guilty asking her family to help keep Zi while she worked. Nia took her hand and pulled it into her lap reassuringly.

"I'm proud of you, though. You're the type of woman that lets nothing and no one stop her," Nia paused, choosing her next words very wisely. "You didn't have the sell yourself to get ahead, but I know that was what you felt was the best choice. You never cease to amaze me, Honey."

Nia paused again, letting her friend digest her words. Then she burst into laughter again. "Somebody should write a book about your ass, though! Some of the shit you do is just unreal."

Both women laughed. Imani in relief. She'd gotten her feelings off her chest. Nia laughed in appreciation of her friend for keeping her life interesting. She let go of all of the anger and hurt she was carrying after that argument with Charles. She knew another one was imminent, but right now she was enjoying her friend's company and these awesome massages.

The pedicurists were drying off their feet and shaking the nail polish they'd chosen off the wall when they signed in. Imani had chosen Passion Peach, fitting for her, and Nia had gone with the cooler Aquamarine. As they moved from the massage chairs, duck walking to the air dryers, the conversation softened. They talked about their children. Nia laughed as Imani told her of her plan to rack up some room service that evening back at the hotel. They didn't mention her sadness or pain anymore. When they were done, Imani paid for the pedicures and they walked, arm-in-arm, back to their cars. When they got to Nia's Camry, Imani reached into her purse and gave her back her phone.

"Now, use this if you need me to come and get you. You know you can come stay with me in the room tonight if you don't want to go home."

"I'm fine," Nia strained a smile, "and I wouldn't dare interfere with all you've got going on." She laughed, genuinely.

"Well," Imani said and laughed with her, but there was a seriousness in her eyes, "you got the key to my house, then. Don't let that negro get your pressure all up, stressin' my Godbaby and shit." Imani sounded every bit of Southside and Buckingham that she was.

"Yes ma'am," Nia said grinning, knowing that all she had to do was say the word and her friend would get Charles' ass together.

"And you don't pop up pregnant with no mud babies, ya hear."

"Oh, no ma'am," Imani dismissed the idea before it had completely exited her friend's lips. "No more babies coming outta this body here. From now on, this vagina is for entrance purposes only."

The friends laughed as they unlocked the doors to their cars.

"I love you, Nia."

"Love you, too, Imani."

They got in their cars. Imani watched as Nia pulled out of the parking space and left the parking lot. She turned on her phone before cranking up her car. Her phone began beeping with notifications. She had twelve text messages and three voicemails. Five texts were from Vincent, three from Steve, two from Zion, one from her married jump-off, and one from her mother.

She decided to read the ones from her mom and her baby now and wait until she got back to the hotel to read the rest of them and check her voicemail. It was the right decision.

Momma: I'm so was proud you for making the decision to put Zion in Calvary and will help in any way that I can.

Imani couldn't remember the last time, even thinking back to her youth, that her mother had said she was proud of her. The messages only got better.

Zion: thank you for coming to see me it was fun! I can't wait to get home.

Zion: I love you, mommy! Good night.

Imani was all smiles on the way back Downtown. She made plans to go to Sous la Terre that evening and enjoy some jazz and dancing.

In Their Feelings

All these men actin' brand new
Didn't want me when I was ready to be with you
Now you're sad 'cause I don't have time
For the bullshit that you do…

She pulled up to the Embassy Suites and let the handsome young valet park her car for her. She walked into the hotel, not even noticing this time if her every step was being watched by the staff. She got on the elevator and rode up to their room. She walked into a room that smelled almost as if it had been sterilized. She laughed, but her eyes traveled swiftly to the place she'd placed her overnight bag. It appeared to not have been tampered with. She laid on her back across the bed and opened the other messages.

Steve: Just wanted to make sure you were enjoying your staycation!

Steve: You've been on my mind all day. I can't wait to get back to you!

Steve: Just an update. I should be back later on tonight or early in the morning. I can't stand another moment away from you. I'll be there as soon as I'm done. Wear something sexy for me.

Imani blushed at how sweet he was being and planned to oblige him. Her defenses were definitely down and she had dropped her inhibitions, too. She was more than ready to experience some new, edgy sex with Steve. She opened the message from her jump-off, expecting a dick pic or some other part of his body.

Jump-off: I been hittin you up and tryin to show you that I want you in my life. Fuck my wife, the way you make me feel is unlike anything I've ever felt before but you on some bullshit. I see you were out for one thing and that's fucked up. I guess you found you something bigger, harder, and less attached to jump up on. That's what you're all about, right? You scared to love and let a man treat you like you're worth something. I see why your ex beat your ass. You playin with niggas emotions like that shit wont make a nigga snap. Hope that nigga eat you and beat it up like I do.

Imani closed that message, shaking her head at the gall he had displayed. Who in the hell does he think he is coming at me like I'm supposed to be at his beck and call? She quickly moved him to the Land of the Dismissed, where men go when they begin catching one-sided feelings, never to return. Sad for him, but Imani had no time or space in her life for the bullshit. Especially from somebody else's husband.

"Save that shit for your wife," she said aloud while opening Vincent's messages.

Vincent: I know we ended on a bad note but I haven't stopped thinking about you. I realized that I'm in love with you and even though the secrets and shit pissed me off, I can't imagine life without you. Please give me a call.

Vincent: I'll be in town this week and would love to go to lunch or dinner to talk. No strings. I just want to see you and make sure you're ok. I was selfish in my actions and want you to know that you being ok is important to me.

Vincent: No response. I guess I got my answer. Imani, please give me a chance to explain.

Vincent: Look, I know this sounds desperate as hell but you mean the world to me. I see a future with you. I was hurt and I know you can understand why. But now that I've dealt with my feelings, I know that you matter more than my ego.

Vincent: I guess I'll wait. I hope to hear from you and see you soon. I miss you, Imani. I love you.

Imani pressed the telephone icon to dial his number. She figured she could at least give him a conversation.

"Hello?" Her greeting was met with his obvious excitement on the phone.

"Hi, Imani! Thank you for calling. I guess you saw the thousand texts I sent," he laughed, nervously.

"It's great to hear your voice, too. I was calling because…" Her voice trailed off because he cut her short.

"I miss you. Like I said in my messages. I really wanna sit down and talk to you. If you wanna be seen…"

"Well, that's why I was calling. I want to see if you'd like to sit down when you get into town to talk about what happened…"

"Well, I can come this weekend if you have time."

"No. No. I'm busy the rest of this weekend, just come as planned and we'll talk then…

"How 'bout Monday?"

"Monday? Yes, Monday is perfect."

"Great! I'll call you when I get there," he smiled into his phone.

"Okay. Okay. See you then," she said, ending the call.

Imani hung up the phone with the case of the giggles. She never would understand how grown men reverted to pimple-faced, emotionally-driven teenaged boys around her. She kicked off her shoes and reveled in the feeling of power that these men gave her. She rolled around on the freshly tucked comforter. She scooted up on the bed and pressed her back against the cool pillows. Taking the hotel phone out of its cradle, she dialed room service.

After a pleasant conversation with a young woman named Tasha, who willingly read the menu to her as she decided what she wanted to order, Imani settled on Chicken Cordon Bleu, rice pilaf and steamed vegetables, which Tasha confirmed was broccoli, cauliflower, zucchini, carrots and cucumbers. She ordered another bottle of wine and a bottle of Life Water. She turned the television on, tuned into Law & Order and waited on her meal. Just as Sam Waterston started to argue The People's case against the millionaire who had been accused of killing his soon-to-be ex-wife who would've gotten three quarters of his estate because of his affair with her twin sister, room service knocked on the door.

Tasha, the same young lady who'd taken her order, rolled in a cart. She filled the room with delightful smells, both from the food and her perfume. She was absolutely gorgeous. About five-foot-two-inches tall, bright-skinned, with slanted eyes, a round nose, and invitingly luscious lips. Her wavy hair hung to her shoulders from the ponytail holder on top of her head, so Imani knew it touched her waist when let down.

She was pear-shaped, with small, possibly B-cup breasts, a flat stomach, wide hips that Imani was sure led around to a full behind, and thick thighs. Imani watched her as she removed the covers from the food, opened the bottle of wine, and poured it into the wine glass. When she looked up and saw herself being watched, she blushed. Not the flattered but disinterested kind of blush, either. The kind that let Imani know she'd noticed her too, when she opened the door to let her into the room.

They small-talked, Imani finding out that she was twenty-three, from Montgomery, and in school for Hospitality Management. Imani invited Tasha to join her for drinks after her shift at Sous La Terre, right down the street. Tasha eagerly accepted giving Imani her number. Imani texted her digits to Tasha's phone. The young lady's back pocket alerted that she got it. When she turned to leave, Imani watched a behind so full and soft it made her want to reach out and grab it bounce towards the door. Tasha opened the door and turned to give Imani a green light that was undeniable.

"See you later," Tasha said coyly.

"You most certainly will," Imani returned her smile, even felt the blood rushing to her cheeks a little.

Imani ate. Enjoying her food, wine, Law & Order and quiet. She planned out her outfit for the evening and debated keeping Tasha to herself versus sharing her with Steven. She would feel Tasha out and make that decision. She didn't want to put the young lady's job in jeopardy by bringing her back for sex with herself, or with both her and Steve. As she chewed, she weighed the options over and over again in her head. Yeah, she'd just wait until later to make her final decision, because Tasha would have to be down for the ménage in order for it to go down anyway.

Imani finished her food and called to let room service know they could come get the discarded dishes. Tasha answered and said she would send someone right up. Imani knew from her tone that the someone would be her. Imani went into the bathroom, brushed her teeth, and checked her appearance. She knew she would be the last stop before Tasha's shift ended and she wanted to touch her. Imani hadn't been with a woman in a while. Not since Taboo, and she was itching for a taste. The feel of soft flesh beneath her, against her, in her mouth. She knew why men abandoned all logic and reason when given the opportunity to feel a woman. And this woman had plenty to feel. She was a supple playground. Imani shuddered just thinking about it. And, as if her thoughts had pulled Tasha to her, Imani heard three knocks on the door.

She opened it to find Tasha standing there deep in thought, biting her lip in the doorway.

"Come on in," Imani invited.

"How was everything?" Tasha asked, trying to maintain her cool.

"Pretty good. Very good, actually," Imani replied before walking up behind Tasha, who was organizing plates on the cart.

"But I'm sure not as good as you're gonna taste to me tonight," she whispered in Tasha's ear.

Tasha gasped and giggled softly. Arching her back into Imani's pelvis and letting Imani take deep breaths of her hair and her neck. Tasha's breathing accelerated as Imani trailed her hands over her body, firmly cupping her breasts, sliding down her stomach and gripping her hips. She turned Tasha to face her and saw the young woman's face was flustered. She had a pained look on her face like she hadn't been touched in a while. Imani grabbed both hands full of her ass and looked into Tasha's eyes. Tasha didn't look away. She met Imani with the same level of attraction that she was being given. Neither of them moved. They both knew sharing a kiss would lead to other things and Tasha was still on the clock. But it was confirmed by this exchange that tonight was going to be a trip. A beautifully eventful trip.

After what felt like forever, Imani released her grasp of Tasha and watched her as she completed the task of cleaning up the food and taking the cart back to the kitchen. Something about all of her motions screamed sexy. Or maybe it was just Imani's perception of them. Either way, she was turned on and couldn't wait until later that evening. Imani was leaning more and more towards not sharing this woman with Steve. Tasha walked, twisting her hips and throwing her ass harder than she had before, towards the door. Imani walked a few steps ahead and opened the door for her. They gave one another a long, meaningful look as Tasha left to finish up her shift for the night.

Double-dippin'

I got a sweet tooth for you
Come let me show you what my tongue can do
Your body has me intrigued
I need a taste of your sweets...

Imani dressed in a blue and black leopard-print mini-skirt, sheer royal blue top, black suspenders, and blue and black leopard-print stilettos. She rolled her afro into a bun, pinning it into place with chopsticks. She took full inventory of her reflection in the mirror, her face perfectly made up with half and half blue and black eye shadow. Her lips were a deep, bronzed-brown. She would definitely turn heads tonight. She picked her black sequined clutch from the bathroom counter and made her exit into the Saturday night atmosphere. She waited at the Valet station for her car and when the young man pulled her car to the curb, she tipped him and got behind the steering wheel heading towards Commerce Street. Once on Commerce, she traveled the block to Sous La Terre, a local jazz lounge.

She knew Tasha was going to be late because she wanted to shower and get dressed for their night out. Imani parked and walked through the open wrought-iron gate and down the stairs to the basement lounge. She showed her membership card, along with her driver's license to Josh, the burly, young door attendant. She paid her ten dollar cover and found a seat at a table for two near the dance floor.

She ordered the "House Special," which was similar to the Blue Motherfucker she used to drink at the Rose Supper Club in her college days, and an order of fries with a side of ranch dressing. Imani munched on fries, patted her foot to the musician's rendition of The Thrill Is Gone and smothered giggles at the white women dancing off-beat. She felt a warm mouth near her ear. Instinctively, Imani jumped and turned her head in the direction of the person who'd invaded her space. She'd been asked to dance half a dozen times in the past half hour, so she expected to see another Caucasian military man with a buzz cut and a case of Jungle Fever to be standing there.

Instead, she saw Tasha in a black lace top and red bra. Her black mini-skirt looked painted on. Her hair was parted down the middle and spilled in big ocean waves around her face, pouring over her shoulders and bouncing down to her waistline. Imani smiled approvingly at what stood in front of her. She smiled even harder at all of the men who were taking in the view of Tasha from behind. Imani knew that the sway in Tasha's back was deepened by her balancing act in six-inch stiletto sandals. She stood up from her seat to give Tasha a hug. Her hands beginning at the small of her back but traveling to the roundness below.

Imani looked over Tasha's shoulder at the onlookers, smiled, and squeezed Tasha's ass firmly. A gesture letting them know that Tasha belonged to her. She let go of her with one arm and guided her into the seat at the inside of the table, closest to the wall. Another territorial move. She motioned to Tony, the server. She ordered another House Special for Tasha, who also ordered a chicken strips basket and fries with ranch dressing on the side. She reached across Imani for fries while she waited for her own food. Her breast laid on Imani's arm, making her tingle between her legs.

Let the fun began, Imani thought to herself, smiling at the fact that she was the envy of every hard-leg in the room. Of course, their male ego's fooled them into thinking they could pull one or both of the women from the other. They would come and ask Imani or Tasha to dance. Do their best with venturing hands, pelvic gyrations, and swift powerful dips to prove to the women why they were the more suitable Friday night date. To no avail. The women never took their eyes off one another. As they teased their male dance partners, their eyes confessed their real interest. After a while, they began to turn down dances and started getting to know one another. They laughed. Drank. Ate. Smoked. Drank some more.

Both of their inhibitions completely gone, Imani revealed to Tasha the reason for her stay at the Embassy Suites. Much to Imani's delight, Tasha was not only nonjudgmental, but offered to join her. This turned Imani on even more. Before she knew it, she'd slipped her tongue into Tasha's mouth and her hand up her skirt. She found soft, warm, clean-shaven lips with no panties. Imani slid her index finger into Tasha's moistness. Then index and middle. Index, middle, and ring. She felt Tasha clench her muscles around her fingers. She felt all eyes on them and pulled herself away from the kiss. She sat back in her chair and listened to the music. The musician was singing Ray Charles' rendition of Georgia. She fingered Tasha to the beat. Tasha fixed the smeared lipstick on her face and maintained her composure as Imani pleasured her beneath the table until she came into her palm.

After a few more songs and rounds of drinks, including two straight shots of 1800, the women began to collect their things to leave. As they waited for Tony to bring their check, Imani took a photo of herself and Tasha kissing and sent it to Steve.

Imani: You said wear something sexy for you. How bout her?

Steve: Wow! I can't wait to get back. You're amazing!

Imani: I try. Lol. Just want to make sure you get your money's worth.

Steve: Is this a package deal or is there an added fee?

She began negotiations to make sure Tasha was compensated for her time, even though she'd stated her willingness to do it for free. Imani figured she would tell Tasha about it later. She didn't see them losing touch anytime soon. Imani paid their check, leaving Tony a twenty dollar tip and got up to leave. All of the men watched enviously as they left, hands weaved together.

Imani and Tasha decided to leave their cars and walk to the hotel because both of them were too drunk to drive. They sauntered up Commerce Street, getting grabbier the closer they got to the hotel. They tried their best to control themselves as they crossed the street to the Embassy Suites. They entered Tasha's place of work, two friends laughing and talking on the way up to a friend's hotel room. They even maintained as they rode the elevator. But, as Imani inserted the key card into the slot to enter the room, Tasha pressed her body up against her and began unbuttoning her shirt. Imani fumbled with the key, not putting it in or pulling it out fast enough for the light to flash green. Tasha was sucking her ear, licking her neck, and had slipped her hand under her bra, tweaking her nipples.

Imani dropped the key card in her own distraction. Before she could bend to pick it up, Tasha trailed her tongue along Imani's cheek, causing her to turn her face and accept the kiss she knew was waiting. She turned her body to share a passionate embrace with Tasha, who took the opportunity to trace kisses down Imani's neck, lifted her bra sucking on each of her nipples before her hand made its way up Imani's skirt, moved her lace panties to the side, and shoved three fingers into Imani swollen, damp self.

Tasha kissed down Imani's stomach and then lifted her miniskirt up around her waist. Squatting in her stilettos, she took a mouthful of her clit. She lifted Imani's right leg up on her shoulder and rubbed her tongue on her clit while fingering her in a harsh, circular motion.

Imani nearly bit through her lip in pleasure. Her leg shook on Tasha's shoulder. It took everything in her to maintain her balance. She was grateful for the door holding her up. After Imani came all over Tasha's face, Tasha picked up the key card, let Imani's legs slide to the floor, put the card in and out of the slot, and opened the door. Imani walked a few steps ahead of Tasha, eager to get to the bed. Both women kicked off their shoes. Imani removed her unbuttoned shirt, and sat on the bed, unhooking her bra from behind and letting it fall to the floor. Tasha stood in front of Imani, fully clothed, mouth still moist with her juices.

She began taking her clothes off one article at a time, beginning with her laced top. She pulled it over her head and dropped her arms to throw it to the floor. Her breasts bounced playfully in her bra.

Yeah, Imani thought, that uniform didn't do them justice.

Her breasts sat up in a red, decorative Victoria's Secret bra. The bra was sheer with stitched flowers and showed fully erect, light brown nipples through its red fabric. Imani was getting more and more excited as Tasha unhooked the bra's front clasp and her breasts didn't move as it fell to the floor. They sat, perky and round, with brown headlights shining in Imani's face. Imani reached out to touch them, she wanted to put her mouth on them. She wanted to touch and taste this woman standing before her, ripe for the picking. Tasha took a step back from Imani, not ready to be had just yet. She smiled, turning to the side so that Imani could get a side view of her ass as she pulled the skirt off herself.

Imani took it all in, a broad smile spread across her face. She let Tasha have her moment because she knew when she got ahold of her, she was going to ravage her. Make her pay for teasing her. And pay even more for just being so damned beautiful. Tasha stood in front of Imani in all of her nude glory. Imani leaned back onto her elbows and motioned Tasha to her with her head. Tasha walked slowly towards the bed.

She climbed on top of Imani, pressing her lips firmly against her mouth. Imani laid all the way down, palming Tasha's ass while they pressed their bodies against one another. Tasha was aggressive. Licking and sucking Imani's ears, neck, paying special attention to each breast, as if she knew they were Imani's spot. Tasha nibbled on her nipples instinctively, like she'd been with Imani before. She traced every line of the lotus tattoo on Imani's stomach before crossing the border to her pleasure zone. Imani enjoyed every lick. Every nibble. Every suckle. And when Tasha took her clit into her mouth again, after pushing its hood back with her fingers. Imani hollered before she could catch herself.

She went with it. Allowed herself to be pleasured by the stimulation and even more so by the penetration of three of Tasha's fingers. Tasha put them in together and then spread them apart, stretching Imani's walls, the middle finger rubbing against her g-spot. The feeling was incredible. Imani came. Faster than she could ever remember. Her toes curled. Her back arched. She grabbed two hands full of Tasha's hair, holding on for dear life. Tasha hadn't paused for a second through the orgasm. She continued stroking Imani's clit with her tongue. This woman is a beast, Imani thought to herself. But she refused to be outdone. She let go of Tasha's hair, lifted her chin with her hand, and looked into her eyes.

"Come here and kiss me," Imani cooed breathlessly. "I want to taste myself in your mouth."

Tasha obliged her, crawling back up towards Imani's face. Imani licked herself from around Tasha's mouth and off her chin. She invited Tasha's tongue into her parted lips for a kiss. She sucked herself off her tongue, wrapping her arms around Tasha's back. Using her legs, she flipped them over. Once she was on top of Tasha, she grabbed her hands and pinned her to the bed.

Imani was slow and deliberate in her attack. She kissed Tasha's forehead, her nose, traced her lips with her tongue. Kissed her chin. Sucked her neck as Tasha wiggled beneath her. She took the erect nipples into her mouth one at a time. Sucked on them, flicked her tongue across them. Licked underneath them. Kissed, licked and nibbled down Tasha's side all the way to her hips before making a trail of kisses along the top of her thigh.

Tasha's legs kicked, her body twisting at the waist. Imani let go of Tasha's arms to grab ahold of her thighs and pressed them down on the bed. She kissed Tasha's second pair of lips, pushing her long tongue deep into her. Tasha's moans made Imani moist. They were also confirmation to Imani that she was hitting the right spot. Tasha came hard. Her walls vibrated against Imani's tongue. She ventured upward to Tasha's clit and began to hum against it. Tasha lost what little control she had left and came again, all over Imani's face.

The two were so engulfed in lovemaking, their moans filling the room, that they didn't hear or notice Steve come in. He stood by the door, enjoying watching Imani bury her face in Tasha's pussy. His erection was inevitable; he'd come out of his pants and began massaging himself to the live action sex scene taking place right before his eyes. Imani had been right about how beautiful Tasha was. She lay there on her back, her silky black hair spread across the bed behind her head, a few strands glued to her face by sweat. Her features, even distorted, were still very attractive as Imani sucked on her clit and maneuvered her lizard-like tongue in and out of her like a penis. Her legs up on Imani's shoulders and wrapped around her neck made her ass spread full and wide on the bed.

Steve had to admit he was impressed. Both by Imani's ability to pull and persuade this beautiful woman to engage in a ménage and by the way she was handling her body and giving pleasure without the assistance of a strap-on or a male organ. Steve saw Tasha's legs tighten around Imani's neck before she broke into convulsions. He took that as his cue to join the fun. He walked up behind Imani who was on her knees on the edge of the bed eating Tasha through her orgasm, and pushed his full erection into her.

Imani's shock showed only in the slight tensing of her muscles. She hummed her pleasure from being entered against Tasha's clit. Steve slow-stroked Imani as she continued to slurp loudly on Tasha, the sound making him so hard it almost hurt. He made sure he pushed all of himself into her, pulled out to the hood of his head and then pushed in again, inch by inch. Imani's slurping, Tasha's moaning, all made for a symphony of pleasure and he was the maestro, setting the time with his wand.

The pleasure of it was unimaginable. Steve closed his eyes to revel in the sensations. He felt Tasha's toes press up against his chest, indicating her nearing orgasm. Almost simultaneously, Imani's insides tightened around him. Their sexual symphony reached its crescendo. All three of them came simultaneously. Tasha's legs fell limp on Imani's shoulders. Imani's body collapsed, laying her full weight on Tasha. Steve, finally opening his eyes, took in the two beautiful women laying in front of him. The situation was almost surreal. But he refused to spend too much time in his head. He wanted to live each moment for the next twenty-four hours. He wanted to feel Tasha. Taste her while Imani gave him head. Watch them perform oral sex on one another while he gave his dick the rest he knew it would need at some point throughout the night. He wanted them both to suck him off at once. Fuck one while using his massager on the other.

While Steve went through his plans with himself, the women shifted. Imani and Tasha both rearranged themselves, getting up on all fours on the bed, and began kissing one another. His dick was a welcome part of the make-out session. It was as if they'd read his mind. His knees buckled at the sight. They took turns, one deep throating him while the other sucked and hummed on his balls.

This is going to be a night to remember, Steve assured himself, holding the back of Tasha's head as she slid him into her mouth. Two women with no gag reflex at his disposal. It would definitely be a challenge. But one that he was without a doubt up for.

The Betrayal

She was too eager
Too willing
Too easy
I shoulda known…

Imani woke up to the sound of the shower running and Tasha's moans sounding off the bathroom walls. She felt a tinge of jealousy come over her. They'd had a great night, everyone satisfying more fantasies than most people can imagine. But she couldn't help but notice the extra attention Steve paid to Tasha, and vice versa. There were moments when Imani felt like one of the toys Steve had pulled out. Just an accessory. She'd tried to talk herself out of it. Neither of them were hers and it was Steve's show. But something in her wouldn't let her shake it.

"There are other women whose pussies are wetter than yours. Bodies tighter than yours. Who know tricks you don't. Ain't had their walls stretched like yours, pushing a baby out and shit. You ain't all that..." Keith's words rang in her head. The lyrics to her insecurity.

Imani got out of the bed and went to the door. She was about to open it, when she heard talking and decided to listen instead. Over Steve's loud grunts, she heard Tasha speaking as he shoved himself into her.

"This pussy good?"

"Yeah!"

"Grab this ass. Spread it. Tell me you like this shit."

"You know I like it."

"Better than hers?"

"Hell yeah!"

"Tell me my pussy's better than hers…"

"Your pussy's better. Oooh!"

"You gone ditch that bitch? Huh? We don't need her here fuckin' up what we got."

"She's gone, baby. I promise. Oh Godddd!"

Imani heard the fall of the water change. She knew Tasha was sucking the life out of Steve by her silence. She heard her slurping and his pronounced moans through the door. She felt her heart beating in her ears as what she'd just heard sank in. She wanted to collect her things and just leave. She was more hurt than she could explain to herself, or anybody else.

Maybe it was just shit talkin', she tried to convince herself. But she knew better. Everything in her was telling her to flee, like she always did. She hated confrontation. But then something snapped inside of her, changing her mind.

I put the two of them together, she rationalized. I need this money. I deserve this money. I sold my body and I'm going to collect every fuckin' penny of it. That lil' bitch isn't gonna move in and take what's due to me. If he promised Tasha something more than what he negotiated with me, then he's just gonna have to pay us both.

Imani didn't know what had come over her, but she liked it. She walked away from the door, got back in the bed, and turned on the TV. She calmed herself and planned how to strategically approach the situation. As soon as she had the plan finalized in her mind, the shower water cut off. She heard muffled speech behind the door. She knew they heard the TV and were probably discussing how long she'd been awake and what she might've heard.

They walked out, Steve first, with a towel tied around his waist and his business face on. Tasha followed closely behind, a towel tied around her head and at her breasts. Imani laughed on the inside, realizing she had the upper hand.

"Have fun?" she asked, slightly sarcastically. A brave smile on her face.

Neither of them knew what to say or how to take the question she'd posed to them. Imani took this as the opportunity to make the best of the situation.

"I knew you two would hit it off. You're welcome." She patted the bed, "Steve, have a seat. Let's handle some business, huh?"

Obediently, Steve sat on the bed. Tasha stood dumbfounded at the foot of the bed, as close to Steve as she could without sitting in his lap.

"To answer your question, yes, I heard y'all in there."

"Well, Imani..." Steve started. Imani cut him off by raising her hand and shaking her head, letting him know his explanation wasn't necessary.

"I think that this would be the best time for me to take my leave, yes?" She made this more as a statement than a question, "You two obviously have no more use for me, but since I did introduce you to Tasha, I think it only fair that you pay me the remainder of what I'm owed and I will get out of the way."

Steve looked defeated. It wasn't his intention for Imani to leave, nor was it his intention to continue with Tasha alone. The conversation Imani heard was merely his responding in the throes of passion. Tasha, on the other hand, seemed to have planned to remove Imani from the situation as soon as possible so that she could benefit for herself. Steve looked at Tasha, then back at Imani, and at Tasha again. He knew Imani had him over the barrel because she had enough information to jeopardize his reputation and Tasha's job. He also knew, because of what she'd heard, trying to talk her out of it wasn't an option.

Tasha's eyes were as big as quarters. The reality of the situation was sinking in for her. She'd gotten cocky and now the tables had turned. Her fate rested in the outcome of the negotiations between Steven and Imani at this point.

Steve said nothing more. He got up and walked to the nightstand, pulled out his wallet, and counted out the remainder of what was owed to Imani. He gave her the additional $1000 he was going to pay Tasha as a peace offering. Imani took the money without saying a word, and proceeded to collect her things. Her calm demeanor frightened her two spectators. She walked out the door without looking back and headed to the elevator.

Imani had mixed feelings about the way the situation had gone. She was relieved that it was over. Grateful she was still able to be paid for the weekend as agreed. But something about hearing Tasha and Steve in the bathroom had hurt. Her mind raced as she exited the elevator, walked to the lobby and walked down the street to where she'd left her car the night before. The drive home was a slow one as her emotions began to get the best of her. Her self-esteem was definitely lower than it was when the weekend began. She chose to view this as a learning experience, but it didn't make it hurt any less.

Imani walked into her house, put her keys on the table by the door, left her bags by the sofa, and went into the kitchen to get a glass of wine. She kicked off her shoes in the dining room, walking with her glass of wine back to the sofa, and pulled her journal from beneath the cushion. She knew that writing would help her sort through her feelings and she really needed to do some sorting. As she sipped her wine she heard thunder rolling, indicating a storm was near. Her pen sat on the blank page. Words eluded her. Her emotions got the best of her and before she knew it tears were streaming down her cheeks. As if the Universe didn't want her to cry alone, she heard the sky open up and water began to pound earth.

She spent the remainder of the weekend just feeling the rain, the sadness, and the reality of what she'd done for money. By Sunday night, she'd gone through two bottles of wine and decided to shower and go to bed early. She had a big day tomorrow. As she shower she laughed, thinking back on her conversation with Nia. Maybe somebody would write a book about her.

See What Sticks

Throw it all against the wall
And see what sticks.
Lingering a sign of longevity…
But it all slips away eventually.

Imani woke up with a migraine and thoughts of Vincent. She popped a few ibuprofen, ate a brown sugar cinnamon Pop Tart and threw on her Betty Boop scrubs, headed to work. Vincent was in town all week and she was excited about getting the chance to see if the chemistry they shared was still there. She smiled at the thought. She pulled out into traffic, heading towards her new job at HospiScript Services. Nia had referred her and she was excited to delve back into the medical field, even if in a call center. This opportunity came right on time. She'd chosen to cut her hours at the auction because this was a full-time position and that meant she would only have to see Steven on auction days.

After the past weekend, she was grateful for that. As she turned off Ann Street into the parking lot of her new job, she decided to let Vincent know he was on her mind. He responded almost immediately, letting her know he would be in town later that evening and was excited about seeing her. After a few texts back and forth making plans for the evening, he wished her a great first day at her new job. She stepped out of her car with a smile on her face and this wonderful man on her mind.

As Imani walked down the stairs to the basement with the trainer and her fellow trainees, she was making plans in her head for Vincent and Zion. She would pick Zi up from school, cook dinner and get her to bed before letting Vincent to come over. Even inviting him in the house while Zion was there was a big step outside of her comfort zone. She never had men in the house while her baby was home. But she decided after touring the facility and as they were herded into the training room, to just throw everything against the wall and see what sticks.

She knew she wasn't ready to introduce them. She just had to hope that Zion didn't wake up throughout the night. Her mind was racing with concern and excitement as a trainer talked about log in procedures and privacy policies. Imani haphazardly took notes as she thought about her divorce decree and how Keith had added a clause requiring her to be dating a man for six months before she could introduce him to their child. He'd managed to maintain a level of control over her personal life even after she'd broken free from him. So, was she truly free? Imani found herself wondering these things for the millionth time since she'd left him.

Damn right I'm free, Imani told herself, not letting those thoughts get the best of her. Even though she had known at the time that the clause was bogus, she was so eager to get away from that horrendous situation that she would have sold her soul to Satan for her freedom.

The trainer was starting in on the names of the medications and the conditions that they most commonly heard of in their profession. Imani had an advantage. Her years as a Pharmacy Cashier at Norman Bridge Drug Store had given her the opportunity to learn from one of the best in the business, Mr. Roy D. Vann, and eventually study to become a Pharmacy Tech. She still nodded her head, appearing to listen. The other, less experienced trainees, were making the trainer repeat herself, anyway. This gave Imani plenty of time with her thoughts.

She had butterflies. She started weighing the pros and cons of Zion being there when Vincent came over. What if they decided to have sex? Imani decided that she truly wanted to try and build with him, so sex was out of the question. Then she thought of the sensitive matter that they needed to address. Discussing her losing their child was a very emotional thing, and she didn't know if Vince was really ready to forgive her and move on. What she felt and truly hoped he would do was be compassionate and apologetic that his actions had caused her to grieve alone.

Of course, she had to take his feelings into consideration as well. The more scenarios Imani played in her head, the more she felt it best that Zion not be there. Then guilt got the best of her. She'd already spent the last four days away from her baby while she tricked out for some daycare back pay and private school tuition. Now, she was abandoning her to try to spend time with yet another man. Just another suitor who may or may not make the cut.

Well played, Keith, she thought to herself. This was the dilemma he intended to put her in. It was nearly impossible not to see herself as a bad mother by having to make this choice. Imani wrestled, rationalizing the situation to herself. Just in time, the trainer dismissed the class for a one-hour lunch. Imani prayed on her way to the break room that Nia was on lunch break, too. As if the Universe felt her desperation, she walked into the break room and saw her friend feeding a dollar into the sandwich machine.

Nia turned towards the chattering of the new hires and smiled as she saw Imani come through the door.

"Hey girl!" she spoke enthusiastically until she saw the wrinkles across her friend's forehead. "Uh oh," Nia's smile faded, thinking something had happened in training.

She pressed the letter-digit combination of her sandwich choice, bought a Pepsi from the soda machine, and joined Imani who had found two vacant seats at a nearby table.

"Imani," Nia started, sounding concerned, "it gets easier when you get on the floor and start taking calls."

Imani, jumping like she'd been jolted from her thoughts, finally saw her friend for the first time since she'd sat down near her.

"No, Nia," Imani reassured her friend, "that's not it. Something else is on my mind."

"I got a penny," Nia prompted her friend spill the beans.

"I'm just torn, Nia…"

"It's not about this weekend is it, Imani," Nia interrupted.

"No!" Imani said emphatically, as if she thought Nia's vague inquisition had exposed her secret to the entire room.

"My bad," Nia put her hands up and surrender. "What's wrong with you then, chick?"

Imani took a deep breath. The look of defeat plagued her face.

"I'm wrestling with my conscience, because Vincent… he's in town this week. I really wanna see him, Nia. I want to see him but, see," Imani mulled over her words, "I've already been away from Zion the past four days and I don't want to keep leaving her with my mama, you know?"

Nia nodded.

"But you know Keith put that bullshit in the divorce decree talking about having to know someone for six months before they meet Zi, so I can't bring him to the house and spend time with my baby…" Imani's voice trailed off.

Nia swallowed the food in her mouth and took a sip of her soda before speaking.

"So, you feel like you're abandoning Zi by leaving her with your mom for you to spend time with Vincent, huh?" she summarized Imani thoughts.

"Yes," Imani replied waiting for her to continue.

"Imani, can I be honest?" Nia asked, a serious look coming over her face.

"Please…" Imani gave full permission.

Nia sat back and laid her arms across her swollen belly.

"Ever since you left Keith and got in your own spot it's been man after man after man with two or three days with Zi sprinkled in there. I mean, I get that you were deprived of sex, affection, and attention by Keith and you're making up for lost time, but," Nia took a second to get her wording right, "friend, I actually think you have your priorities fucked up."

She stopped just long enough for her words to sink in before continuing.

"I know you had Zion young. Hell, we both had our kids young. And I know you had a fucked up childhood. But, I really think you're using these men as a crutch and abandoning Zion in the process. You say you're protecting her, but you leaving her with the same people who fucked you up as a child."

Imani sat stone-faced, listening.

"Now, I've never told you what to do, and I never will. That's not how we get down. But I will say that my niece misses her mama and you're doing you both a disservice by chasing after this validation, comfort, and momentary fixes from these men. Imani, the right man will come along and won't have a problem waiting to spend time with you and meeting Zi. But, until then, you owe it to your daughter to be her mother. And owe it to yourself to face these fucking demons I've watched you run from for the past ten years."

Nia rubbed her rounded belly, soothing the little person who had just gotten a burst of energy from the food she'd eaten. She extended one hand for her friend to hold as she shared her final thought.

"Maybe you should consider talking to a professional. Since I found out I was pregnant, and accepted the fact that Charles is most likely not the father, I've been going to this place, right up the street from here called Samaritan Counseling Center. You can see the intern for free. I see her once a week and she's great!"

Nia squeezed her friend's hand, knowing she'd just hit her with an atomic bomb. "Just think about it, okay?"

Nia held on to her friend's hand. Imani let out a soft grunt, confirming that she heard her. She was taking in everything and time seemed to stand still as Nia's words picked at the scabs of her past. She couldn't even get angry. Nia had only said what she was thinking. What she knew.

She fought back tears. Swallowing the lump in her throat, she got up and went to the vending machine. She stared blankly at her choices. Selecting a Dr. Pepper, she cracked it open and gulped the acidic beverage down. The burn from it distracted her briefly from the reality Nia had just left her with. A reality that had left a bright, red handprint on her ego. She walked back to the table and cleared her throat before speaking.

"You're right, Nia. And..." she was speaking barely above a whisper, "thank you."

Nia looked at the wall clock behind Imani.

"It's time for me to get back to work, babe," Nia announced. "We'll talk later, okay?"

"Okay," Imani confirmed, her mind still digesting. She got up from her seat, hugged her friend, kissed her on the cheek, and walked towards the door to the patio smoking section. She checked the clock on her way out, realizing the entire interaction with Nia had only taken twenty minutes of her lunch break. Guess time did stand still, she thought.

Priorities

The woman in me
Is at war between maternity and the need for love
But she's worth every lonely night
Because she's my gift from up above…

Imani was deep in her thoughts as she cuddled on the couch watching Finding Nemo with Zion. She'd told Vincent, much to his disappointment, that they wouldn't be able to see one another that evening, shortly after her talk with Nia in the breakroom. She'd made some heavy decisions. She needed to spend more time with Zion. She'd been neglecting her baby in her selfishness. And to make it worse, she'd been bringing them into the place where she and her daughter lived. That was just careless.

How could she get mad at Keith for sending his psycho girlfriend to her house when she'd done the same. Nothing had popped off with any of the men, but that was just because she hadn't brought the right crazy in yet. She was going to adhere to the six-month clause, not only because it would give her the chance to see who was serious, but also because it was safer. Something good did come out of Keith's ill-intended clause. The thought of it made her smirk. She looked at Zion who was engrossed in watching Squirt take on the current, her head resting comfortably in her mother's lap. She laughed aloud as Zi quoted the movie.

"Gimme some fin. Noggin. Dude," Zion said enthusiastically, reveling in the bond between the two turtles playing on the thirty-six-inch screen across the room.

The rain tapped on the panes of her sliding glass door. Imani knew it wouldn't be long before it got the best of Zion. Her cell phone vibrated on her coffee table. She ignored it. Tonight was the beginning of a new life for Imani. There were new priorities. An adventure she and Zion would embark on. Together.

****

After Imani got Zion to bed, she sat quietly on the sofa and listened to the rain. Rainy nights were the worst. They were the time when loneliness resonated through the walls of her apartment, in the rhythmic melody of raindrops. On nights when it stormed, Imani couldn't silence her feminine urges with a good book or glass of wine. The thunder filled her with longing. Lightning flashed like the light on a camera, showing her the empty space beside her on the sofa or perfectly flat pillow on the right side of her bed.

Nights like this made Imani want to be held and caressed the way that a woman is when a man loves her. She'd only known that caress once in her life and not as recently as some may think. She was chasing that feeling every time she laid with a man. Some almost got it right, but more out of instinct than genuine affection for her. She was, as she'd come to realize, a love addict chasing the feeling of the first time that you can never achieve again.

Lightning cracked loudly, making Imani get up to walk upstairs and check that Zion was still asleep. She was. Resting peacefully on this rainy night while her mother was plagued with her thoughts and desires. Her sad reality sank in. She needed to sleep, but she just couldn't. She had to face these feelings she'd been avoiding for so long. What did she truly want? For herself? For her daughter?

She was sick of being the one that got away. For once, she wanted to be the one that stuck. She was always a ghost. Stuck in the position of being a fantasy. Being the object, not the norm. Admired from a distance while others, less than deserving, got the time, the effort, and the present. No one was ever there with and for her. She was a getaway, even if mentally. A beautiful escape from the present pain and discomfort. But she started to think she would have to get pregnant to even get a last name. This was the case with her failed marriage and with the women who her suitors stayed with. They claimed to be miserable but after dicking Imani down, they always went home.

There was a time when Imani preferred it that way. Men with women at home were less likely to catch feelings. She saw them when she needed a fix and then sent them back to their women to deal with the real problems. But with Keith being absent in Zion's life, she felt the urgency to fill that void for her child.

She'd always heard single mothers saying they played mommy and daddy, but she always thought that was unfair to the child. There are things a woman can teach a child, as well as things a man can teach a child. Child rearing was a dual person job. Anything else was just unnatural.

As Imani's head swam with questions and revelations, she decided to call Vincent. Her text canceling their rendezvous had been vague. She knew she owed him an explanation.

"Hello?" Vincent's groggy voice answered the phone. In her distraction, Imani had not realized it was three in the morning.

"Hi, Vincent," Imani said nervously, "I apologize to wake you up, I just thought I owed it to you to explain a few things."

"No apology necessary," Vincent responded. "I'd been waiting on your call. I must've fallen asleep watching Dope. What's going on with you?"

Imani was flattered by the fact that he was willing to entertain her, even at this hour. She didn't waste too much time in that feeling though, because she'd realized that feelings like this one were when she had the largest lapse in judgment.

"Vince, I love you," she started.

"I love you too, Miss Jones," he chimed in.

Imani smiled into the phone. "I want to get to know you, more than Biblically," she said jokingly but very serious.

Vincent laughed at her statement. He could sense the nervousness in her voice and that she was not used to being handled warmly.

"Okay," he said encouraging her to continue.

"From what I have seen so far, you have a beautiful mind and an even bigger heart. You're a man who knows what he wants and I respect that. But," she paused, preparing herself for what she was about to say, "I don't know if you really know what you're getting yourself into with me."

Imani could hear the mattress squeak beneath Vincent's weight as he sat up in the bed. He was wide awake now and she knew she had his undivided attention.

"Imani," he started, his tone soft, soothing, "I know very little about you. This is true. But your energy, your spirit is beautiful. I was drawn to that. What happened between us that first night was just confirmation for me that you are just as wonderful as my instincts suggested. But I can also tell you have been hurt, terribly, at the hands of men," he paused, briefly. "And that shit with Keith, and the baby, our baby. You kept your pregnancy from me. For what reason, I have no idea. I wanna be with you. But I have to be able to trust you, you understand, right?" he asked, wanting her to understand where he was coming from.

"I know you being hurt is why you ran from me. But, this is also one of the many reasons I didn't give up. You have so much power, but you are allowing your past hurts to block it. I feel like you're still running, hence your cancellation of our meeting this evening."

"No. I have Zion tonight," Imani interjected her explanation.

"I know that, love," Vincent assured her. "But, in getting involved with a woman with a child, I accepted that you would have her most of the time." There was a hint of frustration rising in his tone. "I have children of my own. I'm aware of your concern with bringing random men around her that eventually fall off. But I'm not in the business of breaking the hearts of mothers or of little girls. I already do it every time I leave my daughters. So you don't have to worry about that with me."

"I just want to make sure you're right before you meet her, that's all," Imani said weakly. "But there's more. I have my own issues I'm having to sort out."

"Hmmm," Vincent thought for a moment before responding, "when was the last time you were loved the right way by a man?"

This question threw Imani off-guard.

"The right way?" She asked.

"Yes, the right way," Vincent repeated, his tone filled with emphasis.

"I suppose if I know what you meant by the right way, I'd be able to tell you when," Imani replied, veiling her embarrassment with humor.

"Darling," Vincent said, not even bothering to hide his disdain, "if you'd ever been loved the right way, I wouldn't have to explain it to you."

Both got silent for a few moments. Imani was trying to regroup from Vincent's last statement. Vincent was regaining his composure. He'd never come unglued this quickly around a woman. This woman was definitely dangerous.

Imani cleared her throat. "Well, I guess the answer is never. Vincent, I've never been loved the right way."

The realization hurt. But she needed to say it aloud. Speak what she already knew.

"Well," Vincent, now calm, tried to save the conversation, "are you gonna allow me to love you the right way?"

"Love me, huh?" Imani giggled at the thought.

"Yes, Imani Jones," Vincent repeated again, "I would appreciate the opportunity to love the woman I know you are. Help you massage away the pains that plague you emotionally, psychologically, and spiritually. And build with you."

Imani was speechless. She didn't know how to take this man. And it frightened her. She knew taking it slowly was wise in this case.

"Sure," was the only response she could muster. She was flustered. She wanted to end the conversation before it went in the wrong direction again.

"So, when will I get to see you?" Vincent asked, trying to get the most out of the conversation.

"Ummm," Imani knew that her response was going to disappoint, "you know I'm in training all week. And then Zion fills my evenings," she paused, trying to see if she could find a way to make time for him.

"Well, let me come over and make dinner for you and Zi," Vincent suggested.

"I can't do that… I mean, it's complicated," she stammered across her explanation. "I would have to explain it to you in person."

Vincent sighed. He couldn't figure her out. One minute she was warm and open. The next she was guarded. He was beginning to wonder if it was worth the trouble. He liked to keep the stress in his life to a minimum and figuring her out was looking like a lot of stress. But at the same time, it was intriguing. He did like a challenge.

"You know," Imani conceded, "Zion will be with her Auntie Nia on Friday night. What do you say we go to dinner?" she offered, waiting for him to decline.

"We can do that," Vincent accepted her offer.

"Great!" Imani couldn't hide her excitement. "Is it okay for me to call and text you throughout the week? You know, when thinking about you?"

"Of course," Vincent's smile could be heard through the phone. "Maybe I can take you to lunch one day this week," he stepped out on this one, hoping she would take him up on the offer.

"Yeah," she said, smiling from ear-to-ear. "I think that can be arranged."

"How about tomorrow?" Vincent's urgency to be her space was undeniable.

"Eager, aren't we, Mr. Garvey?" Imani giggled.

"Just really miss your face and your energy," Vincent confessed, in an earnest tone.

"Well then, it's a date," Imani agreed. "I'll text you as soon as I find out what time we'll be breaking for lunch."

"I look forward to it," Vincent layered his voice with sexiness.

"Indeed. Talk to you tomor... Later today," Imani corrected herself.

"Rest well, beautiful," Vincent wished her a good night.

"You, too," Imani said, ending the call all smiles. She stretched out across her couch and let the storm lull her to sleep. Vincent might just stick, she thought to herself. Only time would tell.

Beginning... or the end

It's beginning to look a lot like...
Forever.
I never thought love was for me...
Could it be?

Their chemistry was great. Imani and Vincent spent every free moment together that first week and texted often throughout the day. Every night they were the last voice the other heard before they went to bed. When he was in town, she was the envy of her coworkers because this beautiful man was waiting for her on her lunch, sometimes whisking her away on his motorcycle, other times bringing her meals he'd made for her and doting over her. He kissed her passionately whenever he left, never being disrespectful by groping her in public. All he saw was her. The women in the room, who may have tried to get his attention, may as well have been chairs because he didn't even blink at their attempts.

She would travel every other weekend to Atlanta to see him. Leaving Zi with Nia or her father, when he decided to be a part of her life. They enjoyed the sights. Went to poetry readings at the Apache Café. Some weekends, they stayed in the house, listened to jazz, and made love all weekend, painting the walls and all of the furniture with the scent of their love. Imani shared her past with Vincent, and he soothed her, making her feel silly for thinking that he would've been judgmental. Over the next three months, they'd grown quite close.

One Sunday afternoon as Imani was preparing to leave, Vincent sat on the foot of the bed. Shirtless, with his black silk lounge pants on, he watched her. Imani could feel that something was bothering him.

"I gotta penny," Imani said, turning to look at him and pressing her back against his dresser.

"Come here, love," Vincent patted the bed beside him.

"Sure," Imani skipped across the room, still in her bra and panties. She plopped down on the bed heavily. "What's up?"

Her enthusiasm was short-lived when she saw the serious look on his face. Vincent wasted no time getting to business.

"We've been chilling quite a bit over the past few of months. Your friends know me. Your coworkers know me. You've met my sister and her children. Even met my girls."

Imani sighed deeply. She knew where this was going.

"But," he continued, "I've never set met Zi. That doesn't sit well with me."

"Baby," Imani began to explain, "I don't feel comfortable with bringing men around my daughter."

"I'm not men, Imani." Vincent snapped, tired of hearing the same explanation over and over again. "I think I've gone through every step in the process to being your man."

"Vincent, I've told you. It's complicated," Imani explained, her eyes filling with tears. "But you're right. You've given me no reason to doubt you. When you come to visit in a couple of days, I'll have you over for dinner. How about that?"

Vincent's expression softened. He'd hoped it wasn't going to take a fight to get Imani to amend her rule. He was glad she'd seen the logic in his argument. He kissed her. Glad he hadn't been forced to go to the extreme measure of ending their relationship behind something so simple. Meeting Zion was inevitable. And, it seemed, Imani had finally accepted it as such.

****

After goodbye sex, Imani gathered her things. He carried them to the car for her, put them in the trunk, and ran around to the driver's side door to open it for her. Before she got in, he held her face in his hands and looked into her eyes.

"I love you, woman," he said with all of the emotion that was bubbling inside of him.

Imani's eyes welled with tears once again. She truly didn't know how to feel right now.

"I love you, too," she said, knowing this was the beginning of a new chapter for their relationship. As she got in the car and backed out of his driveway, Imani felt different. She smiled at the memory of him asking to love her the right way. He was doing a damned good job of it.

Imani had a few hours to kill before she had to pick Zi up from Nia. She loved her friend and the fact that, at eight and a half months pregnant, she was still willing to deal with Zion in addition to her house full of rugrats. She decided to do a little shopping. Heading towards Little Five Points, she parked and walked through the shops, admiring the vintage clothing and handmade jewelry.

The smells of chemical-free incense caught her attention, making her venture into Kloud Nine, a small Rastafarian bodega in the back corner of the market. When she walked in, she heard Redemption Song by Bob Marley and the Wailers playing from a small stereo beside the cash register.

She walked through the store, admiring the cloths and wraps on the racks. One in particular caught her eye. Hanging on the wall was a tan sarong with fringes around the edges. Printed all over it was the image of a lion. His mane was free-form locs. She wanted that for Vincent. A gift to commemorate their going to the next level.

She was so busy admiring the sarong and caught up in her thoughts of Vincent that she didn't notice the man come from the back of the store.

"See sinting yuh like?" he asked her. He was standing so close to Imani that she could feel his breath on her ear. Imani took a slight step forward and turned to see who had violated her personal space. She felt her breath catch in her throat when she got a look at the man standing before her.

He was five-feet-eight-inches and quite handsome, with light skin and green eyes. His sandy-colored free-form locs hung to his shoulders. He reminded Imani of Shaza Zulu from the TV show A Different World. The man was breathtaking, literally. And it was evident in Imani's inability to speak.

"Miss?" the man asked, looking at Imani with concern for her well-being.

"Yes, I do," Imani replied, no longer speaking of the sarong on the wall.

The man smiled at Imani's open flirtation. He extended his hand, offering an introduction.

"I am Prince Dawoud. Nice to meet you Miss…" he introduced himself and waited for her to introduce herself.

"Jones. Imani Jones," she croaked out, her mouth dry.

"Mmm. I was expectin' a mo meaningful name fah a ooman as beautiful an' powerful as yourself," Prince Dawoud said confidently, in a strong Island accent. "Yet ah merely your given name. I am sure, once yuh 'ave chosen a name for yourself, it be much mo' fittin'."

Imani blushed. She wasn't sure if it was because this beautiful man was complimenting her, because of the guilt she felt from flirting with another man less than an hour after she and Vincent had taken their relationship to another level, or a combination of the two.

"Yes," Imani said, "I suppose when I do chose a name for myself, it will be something a bit more meaningful. But, what you may not know is that my name does mean faith, so it may just be fitting enough."

They exchanged smiles.

"Ummm," she struggled to get herself together. This man was quite charming. "I was wondering how much that wrap on the wall was."

"Ah," Prince Dawoud stated, showing his flawless teeth, "Dat one deh is sixty dollars, Miss. It's 100% hemp. Yuh wan me to git it down for yuh?"

"Please," Imani requested.

The man went and got a step stool from behind the cashier's counter. He walked to the wall, passing Imani closely enough for her to smell the marijuana on his skin and mango oil in his hair. He stepped up and carefully removed the tacks from the fabric as not to rip it. His back flexed through his tank top and Imani couldn't help but notice his firm behind.

As he turned to step down and give the wrap to her, he smiled at the way she was surveying him. In her mind, they were naked on the floor of the shop. He stepped from the stool and placed the wrap in her hands.

"Seen sumtin else yuh like?" he asked, standing close enough to Imani for him to feel the sexual energy pouring from her body.

Imani didn't respond. Just took in the smell of him. Her shameless flirting was getting out of hand. She pulled herself together.

"No. Thank you," Imani finally said, stepping away from the beautiful specimen of a man who'd shaken her to her core.

This time, it was Imani's turn to feel eyes on her. She turned, giving him a slight smile. She put the wrap on the counter and waited as he made his way to cash her out. He was in no hurry to get her out of his space.

"Forgimmi fah being forward, Miss," he said as he rang up her purchase, "but are yuh married?"

"No," Imani answered so quickly it made her pull her lips into her mouth, embarrassed.

"Well, a beautiful ooman like yuh has a man, I'm sure," he probed.

"I'm seeing someone," Imani admitted, almost painfully.

"Sad," Price Dawoud said, feigning sadness, "I woulda loved to tek yuh to dinna sometime."

"I'd like that," Imani said, fishing her business card out of her purse.

"Won' hurt none, huh?" he smiled, taking her business card.

"No. It won't hurt at all."

Imani took her purchase and walked out of the store. She checked her watch on the way to her car. She was right on time. She would give Vincent his gift when he came to her house later in the week. Kind of a token.

On the way home, Imani had to deal with her thoughts. She wasn't ready for him to meet Zion, but she didn't tell him that. She'd just make other arrangements. She received a text from a 404 area code.

404-564-3217: It was a pleasure meetin you. Hopin to see you soon.

It was Prince Dawoud. Imani felt guilt pull at her conscience. Here she was meeting and entertaining someone new, when she had a great man like Vincent wanting a permanent spot in her life. She was allowing her fears to help her make dumb assed decisions. She had to get a grip. She spent the rest of the two-hour drive home debating what she was going to do. About Vincent. About Prince Dawoud. About the pickle she'd gotten herself into.

When The Past Collides With The Present

When The Past Collides With The Present
You can run…
You can hide…
But at some point…
Then and now will collide.

Imani's workweek flew by. She'd worked every day at Hospiscript and even made it through the auction day with no drama. Steve hadn't shown up for the first time for as long as Imani could remember. As she clocked out and got into her car, she started to feel the pressure of Vincent's impending visit. The butterflies fluttered in her belly. She hadn't decided what she was going to do about the whole him meeting Zion situation. She didn't want to put her off on Nia anymore because she was so close to her due date and had enough stress of her own. Keith had pulled one of his disappearing acts, so him getting his child this weekend was a no-go. Her uncle was coming in town so her sending Zion to her mother's or her Aunt's was out of the question.

Times like this, she missed her grandma. She loved Zi more than breath and would have kept her at the drop of a hat. It seemed that Zion gave her a new lease on life. She'd found energy to move around that she'd forgotten she had. Imani sighed at the thought. No use lingering on things she had no control over. Her grandmother had been gone almost a year now. Imani chose to concern herself with the living. And she had quite a few concerns. As she turned into the parking lot of her complex, her phone alerted. Before she could put the car in park, it alerted again. She opened the door and walked into her home. She called her Mom and made sure she was on her way with Zion.

They were at Bruster's getting ice cream and then they were on their way. Imani undressed and jumped in the shower. She knew the sugar rush was going to have Zi wired for sound at least the next hour or so. She was going to have to help her burn that energy off so she could go to bed at a decent hour. Imani would never understand the thoughtlessness of her mother, or grandparents in general, giving children things they knew their parents would not allow. But that was the privilege of being able to send the children home. The aftermath wasn't their issue. Imani laughed to herself, knowing that this was payback. Parents got back at their children by spoiling their grandchildren. Zi wasn't a bad child, so even on a sugar rush she wasn't gonna be too much trouble.

When they arrived, Zi hugged her mother's waist firmly before bounding up the stairs to her room. Cheryl handed Imani Zion's backpack and her clothes for the next week that she volunteered to iron because she said it made her feel useful. After a few pleasantries Cheryl ran for cover, leaving Imani at the mercy of a five-year-old on a sugar high.

Imani locked the door behind her before walking up the stairs to join Zion in her bedroom. She found her child sitting on the foot of her bed, her face wet with tears. This both threw Imani off-guard and alarmed her. She sat beside her baby and wrapped her arms around Zi, trying her best to soothe her.

Zion laid her head in her mother's lap, trying to catch her breath from sobbing. When she finally caught her breath, she looked up at Imani through her tears.

"Mommy," Zion said, her little voice shaking, "am I going to live with Nana?"

Imani tried to hide her emotions, which bounced from shock to anger to concern. "No baby," she said, maintaining her poker face as best she could, "where would you get such an idea?"

Zion sighed in relief, her tears slowing down. "I heard Nana tell Auntie that you act like you don't want me so you might as well give me to her. She said all the time that I'm with her, you're not always at work. You do want me, right Mommy?"

Imani took a deep breath, squelching her anger before answering. "Of course I want you, Honey Baby." Imani stroked Zion's hair. "There's nothing in the world I want more than you!"

Zion sucked in another deep sigh of relief. Her tears slowed down and her breathing calmed. Imani started humming and continued to stroke her daughter's hair. After a few moments, her humming escalated to singing. Lauryn Hill's Zion was the song she always sang to calm her daughter down.

She sang Zion to sleep, laying her baby girl down comfortably in her twin bed. She covered her up and turned on the night light, flipping the switch to the main light on her way out the door. She made her way down the stairs and to her sofa before the tears started pouring down her face.

"Fuck you, Momma!" Imani said under her breath.

She felt her anger brewing in the pit of her stomach. She wrestled with the thought of calling her mother and going off. That's why she'd run off like she'd done. She knew Zion was going to tell Imani what'd been said. Imani decided not to let her mother get away with her bullshit. She bolted up from the couch and into the dining room. Her purse sat on the table. She went for her phone.

A chill ran down her spine, making her stop in her tracks. Imani's pulse beat in her ears and her knees weakened. She sat down, put her head in her hands, and began to cry again. This was a different kind of cry. Tears streamed down her cheeks and onto the glass pane of her dining room table. She knew she'd never be brave enough to call her mother and stand up to her. Not for herself. Not for Zion either, it seemed. This made her cry even harder. What kind of mother and protector am I to my child if I can't stand up to the people who've wronged me? she thought sadly.

She felt so weak. So inadequate. She pulled her feet into the chair with her, cowering from the thought. As she did this, the healed over scars on the skin on the soles of her feet veered back at her as a reminder of why she hadn't called her mother. Instantly, Imani was fifteen again. Her Uncle, long gone from the house, the terror of his assaults stopped. But she hadn't had much time to recover because a bigger, crueler creature had taken her reality into its capture.

Her parents were going through a messy divorce. Her father, her only ally, had moved out and she was stuck, the odd one out in a house with her mom and her baby sister. Her mother had begun to take her frustrations and anger with her father out on Imani. Her looking just like him didn't help. Some days she would get beat for what she thought was the weather changing, but usually turned out to be her mother having some angry memory about her father.

She'd started dealing with her emotions by having sex with neighborhood boys who made her feel wanted. The night she'd got those cuts was one of the worst beatings that she'd ever received in her life.

Imani and her cousin Sheena had gone walking in the neighborhood. They'd run into two brothers, Kwame and Walik, at the park across the street from her house. Walking and talking and flirting had led them to the boys' house on Queensbury Drive. Their mother was at work. Kissing on the couch led to sex for hours. Imani was preparing for another round when Sheena knocked on the door and told her they needed to go because they'd already missed their eight o'clock curfew. Imani reluctantly got dressed, not wanting to go home. She never wanted to go home anymore. Everything that she did was wrong. Her mother was always angry. The divorce was making her bitter and Imani was always the target for her misdirected frustrations.

Imani knew she'd be in for it tonight. As she looked at her watch, she realized that not only was it past her curfew, they'd been with the brothers since five o'clock that evening. Imani knew that there wasn't that much walking in the world. She knew she wouldn't be able to craft a believable lie so she opted to tell her mother the truth. There was no point in worsening a bad situation by getting caught in a lie. Halfway home, Imani and Sheena saw Cheryl's sky blue Geo Prism inching down the street. She was looking for them. A chill came over Imani as the car pulled up to the curb and the window rolled down.

"Get in the damn car," Cheryl said, her teeth razor sharp with anger in the dim glow of the street lights.

It was frightening how her mother morphed when she was angry. It made Imani want to run, but she had nowhere to go. She'd tried to go live with her father but he had said, without saying, that he didn't want her there with him. Convincing her that staying with her mother was best, even after she told him about the beatings.

Sheena opened the driver's side back door and got in beside Imani's little sister, Shanna. Imani, frightened, walked behind the car to the front seat. She felt her mother's eyes on her in the rear view mirror. Imani had barely closed the door when she was caught by an open-palmed slap on the side of her head with so much force that it knocked her head into the window.

Imani saw spots when she opened her eyes. Her ears were ringing so she could barely make out what was being said to her. The bits that did come through clearly cut deep.

"...fuckin slutt like your daddy... I can smell the nigga on you... had your ass in the house but you wanna run the streets like a ho... they don't want you... only good for one thing... end up pregnant or with damn AIDS..."

Imani sat silently. She said nothing, not wishing to add fuel to the fire. She felt her little sister's eyes on her and knew she was smirking, enjoying every second. She also knew Sheena was on the backseat afraid for her own life. Her aunt's anger was no discriminator of person. She probably wished she could go home because, even though Cheryl was sure to tell her mother on her, the belt she would get would be a walk in the clouds compared to what was going to happen to Imani. The car pulled into the driveway of their home and Cheryl snatched the five-speed into neutral. She turned the car of and reached back to give Shanna the keys.

"Y'all go in the house and get ready for bed. I'm gonna talk to your fast assed sister."

Shanna and Sheena scrambled out of the car obediently, happy to be out of the line of fire. Imani, whose eyes had been straight ahead, turned to watch them go into the house. As they closed the door, she felt something cold and hard press against her temple. She didn't have to guess what it was, she knew. But hearing the hammer cock back confirmed it for her.

"I should blow your goddamn brains out for embarrassing me the way you do. Everybody knows you're out whoring around. They all talk about it. I can't show my face anywhere because of you and your damn daddy. Y'all are just alike. I should rid the world of one of y'alls useless, sluttin asses. I work too hard to put up with this shit.

Give me one damn reason why I shouldn't blow your head off right now."

Imani didn't say a word. She sat perfectly still, her eyes fixed on nothing. She took slow, shallow breaths just waiting for the nightmare to be over. She knew her mother wasn't going to kill her. She wouldn't have anyone to take her anger out on. But she wasn't going to challenge her, either. She didn't fully know the degree of her mother's crazy.

"I got two good children who deserve their mother, that's why. Your ass is almost out of my fuckin house. I can't wait. You're not worth ruining my life for. I'm just gonna let you ruin your own shit. Get the hell out my car."

Cheryl's words hurt more than what Imani imagined a bullet in the head would have. There were some things that were repeated every time she and her mother got into it. Her not being wanted and being the thorn in her mother's side were some of them. Cheryl's words sliced through Imani's mind like razor blades. No matter how many times she heard the insults, they stung and burned just like it was the first time.

Cheryl put the hammer back in its resting position, making it no longer dangerous. Imani knew her mother had become that much more of a danger. She paused before getting out of the car. She didn't want to be caught off-guard again. After the gun was back in its place beneath the driver's seat, Imani opened the door and got out of the car. She knew the party was just getting started. She had at least an hour of physical and verbal abuse ahead of her.

She walked into the house, her mother on her heels. She paused in the kitchen, not knowing which way to go and not wanting to go the wrong way. She stared at the high-top counter, not wanting sit in her seat there because she'd walked in on her mother having sex with some man there a few days before.

But I'm the slut. Imani thought, not daring to say it aloud.

"Have a seat," Cheryl instructed, pointing towards the counter.

Imani sat in the seat next to hers on the kitchen side of the counter, hoping it hadn't been desecrated like hers. She leaned her back against the wall, facing her mother who sat in Imani's usual seat.

"What the hell is wrong with you, Imani?" her mother asked, trying to sound concerned.

Imani wasn't buying it. She knew there was no right answer to that question. She shrugged in response.

"Where the hell were you? I went to every one of your little friends' houses. Drove through the neighborhood. What the hell were you doing?" Cheryl's questions weren't questions at all.

Imani shrugged again, not wanting to reveal any information. That may've been one shrug too many, because Cheryl stood up and got in Imani's face, dropping the concerned parent act altogether.

"You're gonna answer my question. Where the hell were you?" she asked the question again, slowly. A period punctuating each word.

"We were in the neighborhood. Just everywhere," Imani told a partial truth.

"Don't lie to me, Imani," Cheryl's tone threatened another hand to the face. "I won't have you living in my house that I bust my ass to pay for if you can't tell me the damn truth. I swear I'd send your ass to your damned daddy but he don't want you, either."

"Send me to my daddy. I don't want to be living with you, anyway," Imani's emotions got the best of her and she let the wrong thought slip from her mouth.

"Go pack your shit then, and I'll call him to come get you," Cheryl said, surprisingly calmly.

Imani got up to do just that. No sooner than she had placed her feet on the floor, she got another hit. This time, her mother punched her in the chest, knocking her back in the chair and her and the chair against the wall. She grabbed Imani by the hair and began beating her head against the wall. This time, Imani didn't hear anything that was said. She was trying to free herself from her mother's grasp while trying to shield her face from the blows that were coming from Cheryl's free hand.

She didn't know how long the fight went on. All she knew was that she felt her mother pull up off her and the burning sensation kick in. Her head was pounding. Her face was stinging. Her lip and eye felt swollen and Imani tasted blood in her mouth. She felt something wet and warm running from her eye down her cheek. She didn't have to check to know it was blood. She knew for damn sure that it wasn't tears.

She never cried when her mother jumped on her. Not since the last time her mother and brother, who had moved out, took turns on her with a belt for 'talking back.' She'd looked at their faces and realized they enjoyed the sight of her cowering, crying, and begging their forgiveness from the floor. The next time, she'd taken the beating without as much as a whimper, leading her mom to beat her to the point that she had to wear pants and long sleeves for a week, in May, so no one at school saw the welts and bruises.

Imani found her footing and looked over to see Sheena struggling with every bit of strength in her teenaged body to hold her aunt off Imani. Just feet away, Shanna was standing, taking in the entire scene, not wanting to assist in bringing the beating to its end. She had a smug look of satisfaction on her face. Imani didn't move. She waited until her mother had calmed down and some degree of humanity had returned to her eyes.

"Go take a shower. You smell like fuckin filth," Cheryl instructed, spit flying from her mouth.

She's gone mad, Imani thought as she moved obediently towards the bathroom. She turned on the shower water to let it get hot. She walked across the hallway, realizing there was pain in her legs and lower back. She fought the urge to limp. She collected her underwear and nightclothes and walked back into the now steamy bathroom. She sucked air through her teeth as she undressed and the pain in her body began to register. This was the only sound she allowed herself to make because she knew her sister was somewhere close, listening.

She didn't want to look in the mirror to assess the damage. She just pulled back the shower curtain and stepped into the hot water. She let it hit her in the face, feeling the pain above her eye and opened her mouth to wash the blood from the inside of it. She knew her lip was busted. She felt a knot on her head from where it had repeatedly hit the wall. She had plaster in her hair and her neck and shoulders were sore. Her lower back was bruised from being pressed up against the chair. She let the water beat some of the soreness from her body watching the pink, blood-tinted water run down the drain.

She thought of calling her dad and asking to live with him again, but knew he was more afraid of her mother than she was. And, maybe, Imani thought, her mother's words sinking in, he really didn't want her. This thought knocked the wind out of her. The reality that her father had left and wasn't even asking for joint custody really hit home. Thinking of this made her cry.

Blood and tears stung her eyes. Her sore muscles throbbing even more from her tearful convulsions. She would've given anything to make the pain go away. To get away from this house and never come back. In a moment of desperation, Imani remembered the razor blade she kept tucked in her right cheek. It was a wonder that it hadn't cut her mouth to pieces with all of the hits that she'd taken to the face. This was one time that her mother being right-handed had benefitted her. Imani opened her mouth and used her tongue to dislodge the blade from its resting place between her cheek and gums.

She'd mastered the art of functioning without anyone knowing it was there. A trick a friend had taught her in middle school when she'd gotten expelled from private school and wound up at Cloverdale Junior High. Imani flipped the blade back and forth between her fingers like a coin. She mulled over the thought of slitting her wrists, but couldn't remember which direction would make her bleed out. She couldn't chance messing that up and having to continue life with her mother reminding her of how she couldn't even kill herself right. The thoughts frustrated her. She truly felt like she had no way out. This realization made her cuts and bruises sting even more. She had to do something to make it stop.

All of a sudden, she remembered a story she had read in school where the main character had to swim a long distance and caught a cramp. She bit her tongue to take her mind's focus off the pain of the cramp in her legs. With this in mind, Imani sat on the edge of the bathtub. She tried to decide the best place to cut. A place no one would see. She propped her left leg up on her right thigh and sliced the sole of her foot with the blade. The pain sent a rush through her. She watched the blood flow down the drain. She sliced her foot, again and again, until the pain in the other parts of her body was overcome by that of the cuts on the bottom of her foot.

Imani looked at the cuts, the open flesh of her foot, and realized that she was definitely insane. But the trick had worked, so she was just appreciative of that for the moment. She turned off the water. Put some Betadine on her open wounds, her foot included, put on bandages and her nightclothes.

Over the next few years, she'd cut both of her feet up several times. Never doing both at once, she would alternate between the two. So many things had caused her to feel the need to redirect her pain: her mother wailing on her, a broken heart, her sexual assaults. Anything that seemed unbearable, more mentally than physically, she used as an excuse to mutilate herself. It wasn't until later in life that she'd realized this was unhealthy.

Friday Night

It's the weekend, baby…
And I'm opening up my world to you.
Yet apprehension tugs at my joy,
Anchoring my smile into a frown.

Imani was rubbing her feet and so wrapped up in her thoughts that she hadn't heard the phone ring. But the knock on her door certainly brought her back to reality.

"Who in the hell…" Imani said to herself, looking at her wall clock and seeing that it was half past nine. She had definitely been out of it for a while. She got up, wiping the tears from her face with the backs of her hands, and went to answer the door.

"Who is it?" Imani asked, her voice shaking.

"Vincent."

His voice on the other side of the door shook Imani up all over again.

"Oh shit," she said under her breath while deciding whether or not she wanted to open the door. She'd honestly forgotten he was coming.

Imani finally opened the door to find Vincent with his arms full and an ear-to-ear smile on his face. He held a dozen long-stemmed roses and a big, plush purple bunny rabbit, holding a single rose between its paws.

"These are for y…," his voice trailed off when he saw Imani's puffy eyes and tear-stained face.

"What happened?" he asked, his voice full of concern.

"Long story," Imani said softly, stepping to the side so that he could come in.

She was really not in the mood for a visitor and she knew this wasn't the best time to introduce Vincent and Zion.

Vincent sat the roses and the bunny on the coffee table. He took Imani into his arms and held her as she began to cry again.

This woman has more pain than a Holocaust survivor, he thought to himself as she dampened his shirt with her tears. It seemed like half an hour passed before she gathered herself enough to have a seat on the sofa. Vincent sat close beside her, holding her hand. She hadn't been speaking clearly enough for him to understand any of what was going on. Now, she was looking at the floor refusing to make eye contact with him, apparently embarrassed by her emotional outburst.

Vincent patted her hand reassuringly. He wasn't going to rush her to share, but his broad forehead was wrinkled with concern. After a few moments, Imani got up from her seat and went into the kitchen. She poured herself a glass of Lambrusco and made it halfway out of the room before she thought to pour Vincent a glass, too. She came back just in time to set the glasses on the coffee table and dash up the stairs at Zion's calling for her. The last thing she needed tonight was for her baby to come to the stairs and see a stranger sitting on the sofa. That would've been the icing on the cake of this ridiculously emotional day.

After getting Zion a glass of water and back to sleep, she returned to her guest. Vincent had waited patiently for her to return to him. When she sipped her wine instead of speaking, he followed suit. He knew she was listening for rustling. After she was sure that Zion wasn't going to wake up again, Imani looked sadly at Vincent and geared up to begin crying again.

"No more of that," he said calmly, yet forcefully, "time to talk. What happened?"

Imani sucked back her sorrow, her lower lip quivering. Vincent had to fight a smile. She looked so cute, even in her sadness. She took a deep breath and another gulp of her liquid courage. She started her story with the events of the evening, reluctantly venturing back to her shotgun marriage with Keith, the abuse, the divorce, and the clause in the decree that had been the reason she hadn't allowed him to meet Zion yet.

She only paused to sip her wine and make sure she wasn't overloading Vincent with her stories. Each time she stopped, he urged her on, with a head nod, or pat on the thigh. He looked a lot more comfortable digesting all of the information than Imani felt regurgitating it.

She delved into her parents' divorce and how it had made her the target of her mother's anger. Even showed him the cuts on the soles of her feet. She wrapped up with a timeline of her sexual assaults, five total, ranging from her childhood molestation to the stranger when she was fifteen, the gang rape by the group of Bloods looking for her Crip boyfriend when she was seventeen, repeatedly by her now ex-husband when she was pregnant and on bed rest with Zion, and the date rape drug encounter that had put an end to her partying. Then, she realized that the assault that made her lose their baby was number six. Her heart ached and anger flashed across his face.

Imani finished and although she was fully clothed, she felt more naked and vulnerable than the first night they'd met. She was surprised Vincent hadn't stopped her and left before she finished. She'd barely looked at him the entire time she'd been rambling on and on telling her whole life's story. Her eyes had been fixed on the floor. She looked up fearfully, expecting a look of pity or disgust.

Instead, she saw a look she'd never seen before, at least not directed towards her. Vincent, his face wet with tears, looked at Imani with the most loving expression she'd ever seen. Rather than affirming the repulsiveness that Imani felt, he exuded warmth and acceptance. Before she could catch herself, Imani had leaned across the couch and kissed him. This kiss was the first time she'd kissed a man passionately. It made her feel warm. The way he picked her up and pulled her into his lap. How he wrapped his arms around her waist in a loving embrace that made her feel secure. Like she was right where she belonged.

They lost themselves in one another. This wasn't like any of the other times they'd been intimate. Neither of them pulled at each other's clothes. Instead, they alternated between kissing, embracing, crying and looking into one another's eyes. Vincent absorbed Imani's pain. Her fears seemed to evaporate. She knew, at that moment, that she was definitely in love with him. That he could be it for her. Imani found herself thinking about going back to being a domestic again. He was the kind of man she knew would appreciate a woman pampering him the way she liked to pamper her man.

Imani's heart leapt at the possibilities this relationship presented. She thought this was what joy must feel like and she liked it. He had children so he would be great with Zion. She'd seen how lovingly and carefully he handled his own. Like clockwork, her mind went from happy thoughts of a new family to the divorce decree and the danger of losing Zion if she didn't adhere to the clause in her divorce. Keith didn't want Zion, Imani knew this for a fact, but that wouldn't stop him from dragging her back into court if he caught wind of Vincent before six months were up.

Imani pulled back from Vincent so abruptly that it made his forehead wrinkle once again in concern.

"What happened?" his voice was filled with confusion.

"I'm in my head again," Imani said sadly, "I'm really worried about Keith taking me to court and trying to get custody of Zion if he finds out I violated the clause, ya know."

Vincent nodded, understanding the dilemma. "You really think a judge would take her from you because you're dating me? That's a silly reason to deem someone unfit, don't you think?"

Even as Vincent asked the question, he knew the answer. And the pained look on Imani's face confirmed it.

"It's a term of the divorce, baby," she said, "being divorced yourself, I know you know that what you agreed to in the decree trumps logic and reasoning."

Vincent nodded again, knowing what she said was true.

"Quite a dilemma we have here, Imani," Vincent said, his mind racing searching for solutions.

The next half hour, they weighed options, pros and cons. Imani refused to ask Zi to lie or keep secrets about the relationship. She felt that made it look like she and Vincent were doing something wrong. And she didn't like the idea of encouraging dishonesty in her daughter.

Vincent refused to give up. His determination to be in her and Zion's lives was so sexy to Imani. After lots of discussion and finishing an entire bottle of wine, the compromise had been reached. They would adhere to the clause, much to Vincent's chagrin. What was best for Zion was her being in her mother's care. Equally as important was Imani's mental health, which would be altered by long, drawn out court proceedings. Imani did agree, however, to let Vincent come over after Zion was asleep. He'd have to leave before she woke up though, so they didn't run the risk of them bumping into one another. Vincent made it his business to let Imani know how unhappy he was about having to be a secret and that he was very disappointed to not be able to meet Zion yet.

Imani reassured him that even though her mother wouldn't be keeping Zi anymore, she still planned to visit him in Atlanta as often as she could. Between Nia, until she had the baby, and Keith, who would play Daddy sporadically, she'd make it happen. It meant the world to her that he desired to continue dating her and she was going to spend the next couple of months showing him just how much.

All of that drinking and thinking had exhausted them both. Imani decided to let Vincent stay the night. Taking his hand, she rose from the couch and led him upstairs to her bedroom. She was going to start showing her appreciation right away. A night of sex, an early morning breakfast before he left, and maybe even sending him off with more sex. She didn't know which excited her more: the conversation on the couch, the impending sex, getting to sleep in his arms, or the beautiful relationship that had just been solidified.

When they got into the bedroom, Imani took the sarong she had bought the last time she was in Atlanta and excused herself to the bathroom. She came back, wrapped in it and ready to be undressed. Her excitement was soon squelched however, because Vincent, for the first time since they had met, didn't respond sexually towards her. He even rejected her sexual advances, pulling her into the bed beside him and covering them both up.

"I just wanna hold you. Is that ok?" he asked, pulling her close to him, and burying his face in her hair.

"Yeah. That's ok," Imani said, fearful confusion in her voice.

She settled into his arms, laid her head on his chest, and let her intoxication and his steady breathing lull her to sleep.

Secret's Out

Did anybody see ya
Come into my house last night…
You're my little secret
And that's how we should keep it.

At sunrise, Imani awoke alone in her bed. She got up and walked across the hall to find Zion sleeping peacefully. Her mind couldn't help but be filled with the fear that Vincent had left during the night and that she would find a note on her coffee table telling her that the situation just wasn't going to work for him. It wouldn't be the first time, Imani thought, preparing herself for the seemingly inevitable as she descended the stairs.

Rather than finding a note, she found Vincent, propped up in an upside down position, against the wall of her living room. He was meditating. She couldn't hide her joy in seeing him, but kept it to herself not to interrupt his meditation. She walked through the open living room/dining room space into the kitchen and began collecting the ingredients for a breakfast that was fit for her King: French toast, grits, eggs, and turkey bacon. She was mixing cheese into the eggs while they boiled on the stove and the toast browned in the oven when Vincent walked up behind her. Wrapping his arms around her waist, he buried his face in her soft, matted afro and breathed in deeply.

"Mmm, everything smells so good in here," he said. "Let me step out back and make sure my appetite is right for this feast."

Imani giggled. Vincent made her so happy and knew just what to say to make her feel absolutely amazing.

"Go ahead, babe," she approved, "I'll be out there in a minute."

Vincent pulled away, patting Imani on the butt on his way out the back door. Imani pulled the French toast out of the oven and sprinkled powdered sugar and cinnamon on each slice. She scrambled up the eggs and placed a lid over the skillet to keep them warm. She stirred the grits to keep them from sticking and turned off the eye they were sitting on, putting a lid over the boiler so that they maintained their warmth as well.

Imani washed and dried her hands and went to join Vincent on her back porch. He'd pulled out a second folding chair so she'd have a place to sit. Imani took the wrapper off her Black & Mild and struck a match to light it. They sat, smoking in silence for a few minutes before Vincent turned to face her.

"You thought I'd left," he asked, smoke seeping through his nostrils as he spoke.

"What makes you think that?" Imani asked, thrown off-guard.

"I felt your energy shift once you saw me. You're used to being abandoned, aren't you?"

Imani paused. She pulled long and hard from her Black before answering.

"Yes. I mean, even you left me once."

"And you think I am the kind of man that would leave without a word?" he asked. "Even when I left, I talked to you first."

"I don't put anyone into a category with expectations. I learned a long time ago that you never truly know what anyone is capable of," Imani looked out into the bushes that rested just arm's reach from her back porch. She refused to look Vincent in the eyes.

"Imani, look at me," Vincent demanded.

Imani turned her head reluctantly.

"I've been very consistent with you. Followed through on every promise so far. I am accepting you and this situation with not meeting

Zion even though it goes against every logical cell in my body. The least you can do is not herd me into the category with those who have hurt you."

Imani nodded. Tears filled her eyes. She felt so silly for doubting him, even after he left, he'd come back. She'd never had that happen before.

"Now," he stated taking another hard pull of his blunt, "you're either going to let me love you or please let me know now so no more time is wasted." He blew out the smoke and waited for an answer.

"I apologize, Vince," Imani said. "It's been awhile since I've been in a healthy relationship. I would be honored to let you love me. I only have one condition."

"And what's that," he asked, his right eyebrow raised with curiosity.

"You let me love you back," Imani said with a smile.

"Sure," Vincent laughed, accepting her terms. "Breakfast ready?"

"It sure is," Imani replied, putting her Black & Mild out in the ashtray on the ground. She followed Vincent into the house where he sat at the dining room table. She walked into the kitchen and pulled two plates and two glasses from the cupboard.

She filled Vincent's plate with a King's share of the grits, eggs, bacon, and French toast. Before she prepared her plate, she filled a glass with orange juice and the other with water from her Brita filter.

She took his food on a tray and sat it in front of him. She went back into the kitchen and collected the condiments and silverware: ketchup, syrup, powdered sugar, forks, knives, and spoons. She laid all of this out on the table before going to prepare her plate. She fixed Zion's plate too, and put it in the microwave so it would be ready to eat when her baby got up. When she exited the kitchen with her plate, she was surprised to see Vincent sitting there, food untouched, waiting for her.

"It wouldn't be right to begin without you," he said with a smirk as she sat down across from him at the table.

They both bowed their heads in a moment of silence before digging in. Imani kept her eyes on Vincent while he ate. Even his chewing was sexy. He took large bites but chewed slowly, methodically, enjoying the flavors of her cooking. They both ate until there was nothing left, taking sips of juice to wash it down.

Afterwards, they sipped water, enjoying light conversation about his children and his practice. Imani loved his knowledge of the body, what made it tick, and the importance of balance and how to realign oneself when things got off kilter. She'd only gotten up once since she'd sat down and that was to turn on the tea kettle for their Chai Tea.

When the kettle whistled, she had to pull herself away from the conversation about chakras to prepare the tea. She filled two mugs with steaming water, two tea bags, three sugar cubes, a cube of ice and a shot of milk. When she went back into the dining room, Vincent had made his way to the sofa. She walked over and sat both mugs on coasters on the coffee table. She went back and collected the dirty plates, cups, and utensils from the table. She carried them into the kitchen and began putting them into the dishwasher. She hadn't remembered that Zion was home until she heard Vincent's voice in the living room.

"Hey there, Zion," he said soothingly, "your Mommy is right there in the kitchen."

Imani almost dropped the plate she was putting in the dishwasher. She walked briskly, out of the kitchen, drying her hands on the sarong.

"Hey Zi!" Imani greeted her daughter, excitedly. She hid the fear and concern about the situation before her behind her smile. Zion had never seen a man around her mother other than her father.

"Did you sleep okay?" Imani continued.

"Yes, ma'am," Zion responded, looking back and forth between her mother and Vincent. She was waiting on an explanation. Vincent hadn't moved. He was waiting to follow Imani's lead.

"Good baby," Imani said, moving to scoop her little girl up into her arms. She spun her around, making Zion giggle in delight. She sat down beside Vincent, Zion still giggling in her lap.

"Zion," she started, deciding to go ahead with the introductions, "this is my friend, Mr. Vincent."

Zion stopped giggling and laid her head on her mother's shoulder protectively.

"Hi, Mr. Vincent," she said softly.

"Very nice to meet you," Vincent said, extending his hand.

Zion took it reluctantly and giggled again when he kissed the back of her little hand. Partially relieved, Imani sat Zion on the couch between herself and Vincent.

"Are you hungry, Honey," Imani asked.

"Yes, ma'am," Zion answered.

"Ok, well let me warm up your food and maybe Mr. Vincent will give you the present he brought you."

"You brought me something?" Zion's attention turned to Vincent. "May I have it?"

Imani grinned as she got up to warm Zion's food. She smiled even harder as she heard Zion giggle again as Vincent pulled out the gifts from where he'd put them in his overnight bag.

"Ooh, they're pretty!" Zion exclaimed. "Thank you, Mr. Vincent. How did you know purple was my favorite color?"

"I know a lot about you, Zion," Vincent explained, "your mother talks about you all the time. But what she didn't tell me," he paused, laughing softly, "was that you are just as beautiful as she is."

"Thank you," Zion said, with even more excitement.

Imani walked out of the kitchen and placed Zion's plate on the dining room table.

"Come on and eat, Love Bug," Imani instructed Zion, pouring her a glass of almond milk.

Zion leaped up from the couch and skipped, both arms wrapped around the bunny that was almost her size, to the table.

"Can my bunny eat, too?" Zion asked.

"Your bunny can keep you company but it cannot eat any of your food. As a matter of fact, let's give Bunny its own seat, so it doesn't get dirty, okay?" Imani bargained.

"Yes, ma'am!" Zion agreed, handing her new toy to her mother.

Imani could see in her peripheral view that Vincent was grinning from ear-to-ear, pleasantly entertained by their negotiations. She hoped he couldn't feel the fear radiating off of her. She knew as in tune as Vincent was, he was well aware of her concerns.

As Zion ate and talked to her new Bunny, whom she'd named Benny, Imani walked back towards the sofa. She sat, nervously, next to Vincent.

"You want me to go?" he leaned in and asked, just above a whisper.

"No," Imani said, picking up her mug and sipping her now perfectly temperate tea.

"Okay," Vincent fought back a smile.

"We're in this now," Imani said after swallowing a gulp of her tea.

"Yes. Yes, we are," Vincent said, satisfied with the way the Universe had played things out. They sat, sipping tea, entertained by Zion's conversations with Benny the Bunny.

The rest of the Saturday was filled with the three of them watching Veggie Tales together on the couch. Vincent took Zion outside to ride her bike while Imani put up the clean dishes. She pulled out the ingredients for a roast for dinner.

They walked into Downtown. Vincent pulled Zion and Benny in a wagon. They ate at Smoothies-N-Things, a quaint little café just down the street from the Court Square Fountain. The weather was nice and it felt great to have an outing with both Vincent and Zion. Even though they weren't a family officially, Imani got to see what it would be like if they were.

She'd been so busy enjoying the day that she hadn't thought one time about Keith, her mother, or that damned divorce clause. Not even when they took Zion to the fountain on their way home, where she and Keith had hosted a poetry series one summer. For the first time, she truly felt happy and at peace.

When Trouble Comes Knocking

Boomp! Boomp! Boomp!
Goes the beating of my heart.
I knew it was too good to be true.
I'll never be free of you...

When they returned home, Vincent carried a sleepy Zion to her room for her nap. Imani tried to take her but Zion had pulled away and wrapped her arms tighter around Vincent's neck. Imani went into the kitchen and placed the marinated rump roast and vegetables in the oven. She also pulled out the cornmeal for cornbread, but didn't prepare it for the oven right away. The roast wouldn't be ready for an hour and a half, so she would throw the cornbread in to bake in that last half hour.

She walked out of the kitchen just as Vincent was walking towards the back door to smoke. He had a smile on his face that was unmistakable joy. That pleased Imani. He'd obviously enjoyed their day together with Zion as much as she had.

They went out back together, sitting on the porch silently. The events of the day sank in. This was definitely not how Imani had expected things to go, but in a way she was happy they had. She began making plans in her head to get the divorce decree amended. She would call her lawyer on Monday to find out the process.

Even if she and Vincent didn't end up together, she refused to live under Keith's control any longer. Or anyone else's for that matter. She'd figure out how to deal with her mother later.

Imani came out of her thoughts and saw Vincent staring at her. The intensity in his eyes made her blush.

"I love you," he said, with a sincerity that made her heart melt.

"I love you too," Imani said, unable to hide her smile.

"Today was a great day, huh?" Vincent asked rhetorically because he knew she felt the same way he did.

Imani nodded. Smiling and speechless, she knew that she wanted more days like this. They sat in silent adoration of one another for what seemed like forever until Vincent broke the silence, again.

"I'm not going anywhere, you know," he said sternly, making sure that she understood. "If you thought you were stuck with me before I need you to know that you're really stuck with me now."

"Is that so?" Imani asked coyly. "Or is it that you're stuck with us now?" she asked earnestly.

"I don't mind being stuck with a woman and a child that make me feel as wonderfully as the two of you do," he responded, smiling harder than before.

Imani giggled, knowing he meant every word. She excused herself to the kitchen to check on the roast. She was pouring the cornmeal into the mixing bowl when someone startled her by beating on the front door. Before Imani could get out of the kitchen Vincent was back in the house, walking in long strides towards the door. They'd barely made it across the living room when a familiar voice boomed on the opposite side of the door.

"Answer the damn door, Imani," Keith yelled in between pounds.

"Oh shit," Imani said more to herself than to Vincent. "What the hell does this idiot want?"

"I know you got a nigga in there with my baby. John said he saw y'all playing family and shit," Keith said, his speech slurred.

Imani knew he'd been drinking, which always meant trouble. Imani looked at Vincent who was standing in full protector mode waiting for her to open the door. Imani touched his forearm to calm him but was afraid he could feel the fear permeating through her fingertips.

"Keith, go home!" she yelled, thinking of her neighbors and not wanting to bring drama to her nice, quiet community.

"I ain't going nowhere. I told you about hoeing around with my baby in the house. Open the door. I wanna see the punk ass nigga who's fuckin' my wife and trying to play daddy to my damn child," Keith yelled back, beating on the door again.

Imani knew it was only a matter of time before the courtyard would be filled with spectators wanting to know who and what was the cause of their Saturday afternoon being disrupted. If Keith kept this up, Imani knew both the landlord and the police would be called. She cared nothing about the police, but Imani couldn't risk getting evicted because of Keith's foolishness.

She was torn between opening the door and calling the police herself. She didn't want any more trouble and hoped that by opening the door, the issue could be resolved calmly. She looked back at Vincent. He gave her a slight head nod, telling her it was okay to open the door.

"Okay Keith, I'm gonna open the door, but you have to come in here and act like you got some sense," she explained, her voice trembling a little.

She knew Keith and sense were like oil and water. Still, him being in her house was better than him cutting the fool outside the door.

"Fine," he huffed, "open the door."

Imani removed the chain and dead bolt from the door. She opened the door to find a sweaty Keith on her porch.

"Come on in, Keith," she stepped back so he could enter the house.

She looked past him to see several of her neighbors standing outside of their doors, watching the spectacle. She closed the door to see Keith sizing Vincent up. He was prepared to take on the man who was taking his place until he saw Vincent, almost a foot taller and fifty plus pounds heavier than him. Vincent's stance told that he was ready to defend Imani, Zion, and the house they were standing in. So instead, Keith turned his aggression towards her.

"So you're a domesticated bitch now, huh?" Keith spat, smirking as the insult slapped Imani in the face. He turned his back to Vincent completely.

Vincent's face twitched, but Imani slightly shook her head signaling that she had it under control.

"What do you want, Keith?" Imani asked, suddenly feeling empowered with Vincent there.

"I wanted to see for myself that you call yourself trying to reconstruct yourself a family. What you think this shit is, just add a nigga and stir?" Keith snickered at his own joke.

He smelled of Vodka. Imani hated that smell on him because it used to mean that she was gonna get her ass kicked. She felt the fear come over her like it had so many times when they were married, but this time she didn't let it consume her.

Keith took a step closer but Imani didn't flinch. Behind him, she saw Vincent's jaw tighten and folds appear in his forehead. He didn't move, though. She could tell he knew that this was her battle but the slightest motion from her would be all he needed to step in.

"Keith," she said, as calmly as possible, "I think you should leave. You're drunk and this could go wrong in so many ways. Zi is upstairs napping. I don't want you to wake her with your ruckus. She doesn't need to see you like this. Please…"

"So, now you're worried about Zi? You got this nigga all in the apartment playing house and shit with my child and I need to go?" Keith spat, interrupting her. "I ain't going no damn where. How 'bout you and your trick," he said motioning slightly behind him towards Vincent, "make me leave."

"Baby, all you gotta do is say the word and I'll throw him out on his ass," Vincent said, speaking for the first time since Keith had come in the door.

"No," Imani said, "I got it, Vince." She looked past Keith lovingly at Vincent. Her eyes told him that she was fine. That she needed to do this.

"That's right. Keep your dog in check," Keith said arrogantly. "You know why she won't let you throw me out? Because no matter how good you dickin' her down, she's always gonna be my bitch," Keith sneered, addressing Vincent with his back remaining to him in an act of blatant disrespect. His eyes never left Imani.

"Go 'head. Tell him. You're my bitch. This is my house. Can't nobody replace me," he said, provoking Imani with insults.

Vincent's fists clenched at his sides. He was getting angry. He'd had about enough of Keith and his bullshit.

Imani's jaw tightened. She'd heard enough as well.

"Keith," she said with a sternness she'd never used with him, "it's time for you to go. I'm sick of you. Been sick of the drama and bullshit for years. You're no longer welcome around me and my daughter. So get the fuck…"

WHAP!

Before she could complete her statement, Keith's boxing training manifested in a quick, hard right cross connecting with her jaw. Imani saw red as the blow knocked her to the ground. She looked up from the floor to see Vincent grab Keith up into a basket hold.

More disturbing than the scene of her man snatching her ex-husband up off his feet was the sound of Zion's scream from the top of the stairs.

"Daddy no!" Zion yelled, her little voice piercing the tense air in the room.

"Mommy!" A shrill scream was followed by Zion flying down the stairs as fast as her little legs would take her. She stumbled, midway the stairway. Her tiny butt bumped the rest of the way to the first floor.

When Zion reached the bottom of the stairs, she didn't pause to tend to her own wounds. Instead, she regained her footing and raced over to her momma.

"Daddy," Zion fumed in her father's direction, anger that Imani had never seen come from her baby. "You don't hit Mommy. Boys don't hit girls!"

She wrapped her arms around her mother's neck and continued glaring angrily at her father. The sight of him being restrained by Vincent, both arms crossed firmly across his front, his hands held firmly behind his back, seemed to have no impact on Zion at all. Keith struggled for freedom to no avail, but the hopelessness seemed to do nothing to stop him from trying. He was sweating. Imani was unsure if this was from the struggle, the liquor, or both.

Then, there were three heavy knocks on the front door. She didn't have to ask who it was because she knew someone had called the police with all of the noise that had gone on before and after she'd let Keith into the house. She got up slowly, feeling the swelling in her face and the soreness from her fall onto the hardwood floor. She limped to the door, her right hip hurting terribly from the landing. She looked over at Vincent who hadn't broken a sweat or his grip on Keith and mouthed the words, "thank you."

Black and Blue

What are we fighting for?
Why can't we make love not war?
You beat my heart until you made it
Black and blue. Black and blue.

Imani opened the door to find two police officers, one tall slender white male with long, brown hair, longer than Imani thought would be acceptable for MPD. The other was a short, petite black female with a Caesar fade so clean that she should refer her partner to her barber.

"Ma'am," the female officer said calmly, "we received a call about a disturbance at this residence. Is everything okay?"

Imani knew the question required no answer. She just pulled the door further open and stepped back so the officers could see the scene that was going on in her living room. Zion was still sitting on the floor by the stairs, next to small splatters of blood that must have come from Imani's mouth when she fell. Her eyes were still fixed angrily on her father. She was rubbing her back and her legs from her fall down the stairs.

The arrival of the police hadn't stopped Keith from attempting freedom. It hadn't been cause for Vincent to let him go, either. The officers shot one another a look before the male asked if they could come in. Imani nodded, stepping to the side so they could enter and quickly closed the door behind them. She was trying to spare herself of any more embarrassment with her neighbors. The officers introduced themselves. The male officer, as Timbres, and the female as Alexander.

"Sir," Officer Timbres addressed Vincent, in a nasal voice and strong Southern accent, "could you let him go, please?"

Vincent paused briefly before complying, looking over at Imani who gave him the go ahead. When he let Keith go, everyone was directed to sit down so the officers could get an idea of what'd gone on. Imani and Vincent sat on separate ends of the couch. Keith was directed to sit in the Papasan chair by the window. His eyes were fixated on Vincent because Zion had chosen to sit beside him. She was laying her head on his arm and he was rubbing her hair soothingly. No one would believe that they'd just met for the first time today by the way they were interacting.

Imani was giving her a statement to the officers and hadn't noticed Vincent and Zion. It wasn't until she was asked who everyone was that she saw the two of them. The sight warmed her heart and even made her forget the pain in her face for a moment. The sight of Keith looking at them with eyes full of daggers was the next thing she saw. Imani had to stifle laughter as she told them who he was. He really looked like a child mad at his parents for putting him in time-out.

That was the moment it all came together for her. He was just a child stuck in a grown-up body. Still the little boy who'd seen his dad beat his mother up when he was eight years old. All those beatings she endured were temper tantrums from a child who'd never been taught how to express his feelings properly. Imani almost felt sorry for him. But this time, she wasn't going to lie for him like she'd done so many times when they were married. Lies about being clumsy and falling to hide the fact that he'd taken a fist to her face, or chest, or wrapped his hands around her neck. This time, she was going to stand up for herself and Zion and tell the truth. Her face told half of the story anyway.

She recanted the events of the incident to the police. Explaining that she'd let Keith in hoping to be able to have a civilized conversation and so he wouldn't continue to disturb her neighbors. Told them that Keith had hit her when she, seeing that civil conversation couldn't be had, told him to leave. Vincent, she explained, had restrained him to prevent him from hitting her again. When she mentioned that Zion had stumbled down the stairs rushing to her side, Officer Alexander walked away to make a phone call.

They interviewed Vincent, whose description of events matched Imani's, almost as if they'd planned it. It wasn't until they got to Keith that things got interesting.

"Tell us what happened, Mr. Jones," Officer Alexander asked after completing her call.

"This man is in here with my wife," Keith stated emphatically.

"So, you're married to Mrs. Jones and Mr. Garvey was here with her?" Alexander asked, a bit confused.

Imani shifted, ready to interject, but Officer Alexander held her hand up instructing her to keep quiet.

"No, we're not married. We're divorced. But she's gonna come back to me, I know it. So this nigga ain't got no business in here with her. Trying to play husband and daddy to my baby," Keith explained, as if what he was saying made sense.

"Do you live here, Mr. Jones?" Officer Timbres asked, trying to make sense of the situation.

"No, I don't," he said, becoming frustrated with the line of questioning, "but my family does," he said, speaking to the Officers slowly as if they were the ones with the problem comprehending.

A knock on the door cut into the awkwardness that had filled the room. It startled Imani and Zion, but Officer Alexander walked to the door like she was expecting someone.

"Officer Alexander?" The average height, plump white woman with a salt and pepper bun pinned loosely at the top of her head asked, making sure that she was in the right place.

"Yes," Alexander confirmed, motioning for Imani to join her at the door.

Confused, Imani rose from her seat and walked across the room to the door.

"Miss Jones," the woman said, shifting the file folder and legal pad that were pressed against her chest under her left arm so she could extend her right hand. "My name is Sarah Armstrong. I'm a Child Services Case Worker from the Department of Human Resources."

Imani's breath caught in her throat and her heart dropped. She was about to lose her baby. She looked fearfully back and forth between Alexander and Armstrong.

Seeing Imani's fearful expression, Mrs. Armstrong offered reassurance.

"You're not in trouble, Miss Jones. And I didn't come here to take your daughter. Officer Alexander called me because it's procedure when abuse happens and a child is involved. She can't interview your daughter without me present."

She looked calmingly at Imani. "May I come in?"

Imani nodded nervously. She was filled with fear, anger, and guilt. She'd heard stories of what happened to children when DHR got involved. Why did let Keith in? Why did I let Vincent meet Zion? Why did I let him wear her down when I knew what was in the divorce decree? Her mind was running a mile a minute as she escorted Mrs. Armstrong to the dining room table so they could talk and get the paperwork done before she interviewed Zion.

As they sat down, Mrs. Armstrong began organizing the papers. The timer beeped on the oven, letting Imani know her roast was done.

She excused herself to take the roast out of the oven. She took the time to embrace some degree of normalcy. Busying herself with making sure the roast and vegetables were done, she put her cornbread in the oven and hoped this nightmare would be over before the food got cold. She chose, with that thought in mind, to get Zion's interview over with as quickly as possible so she could get Keith and these suits out of her house.

When she sat back down, there were four forms for her to read and sign: one explaining the process, another giving consent for the Social Worker to interview Zion without her, another advising her of her rights, and the last explaining that there would be regular visits over the next six weeks with the Social Worker to make sure Zion was readjusting to life properly after the traumatic event.

Mrs. Armstrong also explained that she may recommend additional counseling for Zion and it would be provided free of charge. It was all too much for Imani. But she knew she had to keep herself together because Zion would panic if she saw that her mother was frightened.

She looked over to see Vincent watching her. The caring in his eyes let her know that he could feel her concern and was there for her. Just slightly behind him was Keith, who could also feel her fear, seized the opportunity to make matters worse.

"Make sure you tell her about the divorce decree," he stopped mid-interview with Officer Timbres to yell across the room.

"She's not supposed to have anybody she's fuckin' around with around my baby until she's known them six months," he explained to the Officers.

"I know you ain't known him six months," he directed at Imani again.

He was making things worse and worse. As if Imani's swollen face and busted lip weren't enough, his incoherent explanation and the use of foul language in front of Zion painted the perfect portrait of dysfunction.

Imani looked at Mrs. Armstrong apologetically. To her surprise, the social worker's face was covered with compassion. This was one time that Imani didn't have a problem with someone feeling sorry for her. She felt sorry for herself.

"Am I going to lose my baby?" Imani asked quietly so Zion couldn't hear.

"I can't make any promises, Miss Jones," Mrs. Armstrong answered honestly, matching Imani's discreet tone. "Why don't you show me to Zion's room and let me talk to her there for a little while. Let's get her away from this situation, allow the police to handle Mr. Jones, and we'll talk after things have calmed down, okay?"

Imani agreed, getting up and leading Mrs. Armstrong back into the living room.

"Zi Baby," Imani spoke softly and calmly to her child, "this is Mrs. Armstrong. She wants to talk to you about what happened today, okay?"

"Yes, ma'am," Zion said, moving off the couch and away from Vincent. "Be right back," she said to him before limping towards her mother.

Imani picked her up and carried her up the stairs to her room. Mrs. Armstrong followed close behind.

"I love you, Zi. See you later," Keith yelled up the stairs behind them.

Zion's only acknowledgment that she had heard him was her laying her face in her mother's chest.

"We're gonna make your butt-butt feel better after we eat dinner, okay? You can't take medicine on an empty stomach," Imani promised her baby.

"Yes, ma'am," Zion responded softly, looking at her mother's swollen face.

"I'm gonna be okay too, Zion," Imani assured her baby. "Are you alright?" she asked.

"I'm okay, Mommy," Zion said, looking at Mrs. Armstrong.

"Wanna sit on my bed with me?" she invited the Social Worker, picking up Benny the Bunny and sitting him on her lap.

"Sure," Mrs. Armstrong smiled at the polite invitation. "I'd love to."

As she sat down, Imani took her leave. The last thing she heard was Zion telling Mrs. Armstrong that her Bunny's name was Benny and Mr. Vincent had given him to her. She knew there was nothing more that she could do. She had to allow the interview to take place and go from there. She walked back down the stairs, her hip hurting worse the more she walked on it. She knew carrying Zion hadn't helped, but she wasn't going to let her baby walk in pain to avoid hurting herself.

Keith was still explaining the situation to the officers who, at this point, showed no hope of making sense of what he was saying. They just took notes half-heartedly. Vincent stood as she made her way down the stairs, braced to run and catch her in case she stumbled. Officer Timbres, who was closer, walked towards the stairs, offering his arm to help her down the last few steps.

"Miss Jones," he said, still assisting her, "I need to take some pictures of your injuries."

He pulled a slim, silver camera from his front shirt pocket and took four photos. Two were of Imani's front profile, and one from either side. Officer Alexander walked up the stairs to check on Zion and Mrs. Armstrong and to get Zion's statement. When she came down alone, Imani knew they'd agreed to keep Zion in her room so she didn't see what was about to happen.

"Mr. Jones," Officer Timbres said, reaching into the pocket on the back left side of his utility belt, "would you stand up for me, please?"

Keith's face was shadowed with defeat as he obliged.

"Put your hands behind your back please," Officer Timbres requested.

"You have the right to remain silent. Anything you say can and will be used against you in a court of law. You have the right to an attorney. If you cannot afford an attorney, one will be appointed to you..."

As he placed the silver bracelets on Keith's wrists, he recited Keith's Miranda Rights and his partner opened the door. Keith was led out and across the courtyard with Imani's neighbors looking on.

"Miss Jones," Officer Alexander said, before following them to the cruiser, "you can follow us Downtown to sign a warrant. But if you choose not to, the City will press charges on your behalf."

She looked to the cruiser, where Keith's head was being lowered into the car and over to Vincent before she made her final statement.

"Ma'am, most of what he said didn't make much sense. But that statement about the divorce decree he mentioned several times. And now that DHR is involved, you want to make sure that you have your paperwork in order. You know what I'm saying? I would strongly advise you to sign a warrant and consult with an attorney. I'd hate for you to lose custody of that sweet little girl to him because you didn't cover your bases," Officer Alexander offered her advice.

Imani nodded her understanding. She was silenced by fear.

"Good night, ma'am," Officer Alexander said loudly enough for Mrs. Armstrong to hear her. An obvious cue. "Sir," she addressed Vincent.

Imani nodded again. Still unable to speak. Vincent walked up behind her and placed his arm around her shoulder in an attempt to comfort her. They watched from the open door as she got in the cruiser and it pulled off. They closed the door and Vincent escorted a trembling Imani to the couch.

A few moments later, Mrs. Armstrong and Zion descended the stairs. Imani had kept herself together because she didn't want her baby to see her upset. She forced a smile as Zion jumped off the last step and ran to her, bounding into her lap, showing no pain from her fall. Imani didn't even grimace in pain when Zion's knee caught her on her sore side.

Zion gave her the tightest hug her little body would allow. It felt like she was trying to squeeze all of the pain out of her mother's pores. Imani closed her eyes tightly, and allowed herself to feel her baby's love for her. When she opened them, she saw Mrs. Armstrong smiling at her.

"Miss Jones, may I have a word with you in private?" Mrs. Armstrong asked, pleasantly.

"Sure," Imani agreed, sliding Zion onto the couch beside Vincent. "Baby, you and Vincent watch Veggie Tales while I get dinner setup and talk to Mrs. Armstrong, okay." She got up and led the way to the kitchen.

Imani began to pull out the plates, glasses, and silverware, and set the table. She went back into the kitchen to tend to the food, pulling the cornbread out of the oven. Mrs. Armstrong took the opportunity to fill her in on the conversation with Zion and the next steps in the process.

"Zion is very intelligent. She's very well-loved and aware of everything that has gone on between you and her father," Miss Armstrong explained with joy in her tone. "She's a very resilient child and loves both of you very much but," she paused, preparing to begin with the bad news, "she's very angry with her father. She knows that what he's doing is wrong because you taught her that it is. She also told me about what your mother said."

Mrs. Armstrong looked at Imani with a saddened expression. Imani looked away embarrassed and busied herself with venturing from the kitchen to the dining room setting up dinner. When she finished she stood with her back pressed against the sink, bracing herself for the remainder of the debrief.

"Ahem," Mrs. Armstrong cleared her throat. No matter how many times she did this, she hated the part of her job that involved telling the parents what their children had said, usually because the children never came to the parents as openly as they did her. Luckily for Imani, she wasn't going to lose her child to Protective Services like some mothers in similar situations.

"Zion likes Vincent a lot," she started, "she told me that she just met him for the first time today."

Imani nodded her head up and down in response to the question, although she knew it was rhetorical.

"Yes, ma'am," Imani replied, "there's a clause in my divorce decree with Keith that says I have to know a man for six months before he can meet Zi."

"And you've known Mr. Garvey for six months?" Mrs. Armstrong asked.

"No," Imani looked at the floor. "He wasn't supposed to meet Zion today. He came by to see me and she woke up from her nap early."

"Mmm hmmm," the social worker replied.

She met eyes with Imani whose desperation was all over her face. She seemed to be searching for an answer that wouldn't result in some life-altering decision.

"Miss Jones," Mrs. Armstrong said, "that's going to be a matter for the courts. My job is to make sure Zion isn't living in a dangerous environment because of the nature of the incident."

She paused, giving Imani the chance to digest what she was saying, which was confirmed by a deep sigh of relief.

"It's my observation that Zion is a very happy, healthy, loved child. She has a firm grasp of right and wrong and has no problem expressing her concerns, which shows that you encourage that. You seem to be the victim of emotional and physical abuse at the hands of loved ones, but it appears you've broken that cycle with your daughter. I commend you for that," she smiled broadly at Imani.

"Thank you," Imani squeaked out.

"I would recommend you consulting with an attorney about that clause because I have a feeling Mr. Jones is going to pursue obtaining custody of Zion. I'll be making regular visits here and at Zion's school. You'll get a copy of my final report for your records. And I will, if needed, be happy to testify at any court proceedings," she smiled again, knowing that even in the good news Imani was rattled. No one liked having their lives invaded by strangers.

Imani returned the closest thing to a smile she could muster. Her life was now under a microscope. Now she knew how bacteria felt. She knew she was a good mother. But now it was going to be up to others to confirm that she was in order for her to continue raising her daughter.

"Would you like to stay for dinner?" she invited, letting Mrs. Armstrong know that she was interrupting her routine.

"Thank you, but I can't," Mrs. Armstrong declined. "I have to get home. I'm sure my husband thinks I've fallen off the edge of the Earth. But it sure does smell good." The women exchanged a polite giggle before Imani escorted Mrs. Armstrong to the front door.

"See you later, Zion," Mrs. Armstrong said.

"Bye," Zion said, her eyes never leaving the TV screen.

"Mr. Garvey," she said to Vincent, as he stood to shake her hand, "it was a pleasure."

"Likewise," Vincent said shaking her hand firmly.

Imani opened the door for Mrs. Armstrong and gave a faint smile good night.

"I'll be in touch," Mrs. Armstrong said, crossing the threshold into the outside world.

"Yes, ma'am," Imani said, anxious for this woman to leave her home. She watched to make sure that she got into her car safely and out of the parking lot before closing her front door.

"Who's hungry?" she asked, excited to only have her daughter and Vincent in her home.

"Me!" Zion and Vincent said in unison.

"Let's eat," Imani declared as the three of them made their way to the dinner table.

A Couple of Forevers

It can get hot
Then it gets rough
It can get crazy
But not for us…

After dinner, Vincent washed dishes while Imani bathed Zion and got her ready for bed. She read Chick-a Chick-a Boom Boom to her and kissed her goodnight.

"Mommy," Zion said, as Imani flipped the light switch on her way out the door of her bedroom.

"Yes, baby?" Imani stopped in her tracks.

"Tell Mr. Vincent goodnight and thank you," she requested yawning.

"I sure will," Imani promised, a smile lighting up her face.

When Imani got downstairs, Vincent had finished the dishes, dimmed the lights and had a glass of Lambrusco waiting for her on the coffee table. She sat on the sofa beside him and took a gulp of the crimson liquid. She looked at him with an embarrassed smile.

"Today was an eventful day, huh?" she asked, trying to gauge his feelings about the course of events that had occurred.

He let out a booming laugh. "Eventful is one way to describe it," he said, his face lit up with a smile. "How you feeling?" he asked her, looking at her beautiful face still swollen from the lick she'd taken.

Imani reached up and touched her face, embarrassed even more. She gulped her wine again before answering.

"I don't think Zion is all the way asleep. Wanna join me outside for a smoke?" she asked, getting up from the sofa.

"Sure," Vincent agreed, standing up as well.

They walked out the patio. Imani pulled out and lit her Black & Mild while Vincent rolled a joint. After they'd both calmed their nerves, Imani turned away from the trees and met eyes with Vincent.

"Honestly, baby," she started, choosing to lay it all on the line, "I'm nervous, afraid, embarrassed and elated all at the same time."

Vincent nodded his head, validating that all of those were relevant emotions.

"Even though I'm thrilled that you and Zi got to meet one another, I'm pretty sure my life is about to get a lot harder than it already is," she stated the obvious to him. "And I can't help but think that you're about to go back to Atlanta, to your life, and I'm going to be left here to sift through all of this shit."

The last statement hit Vincent unexpectedly. Imani could see the impact of it in his frown, furrowed brow and tightened jaw. This made Imani stop talking. She didn't think that would upset him. She didn't intend to imply that she thought he was going to abandon her. She searched for the words that would correct things but her mind was mush. She began to panic because she knew she couldn't have an argument right now. Her heart couldn't take it. Before she could say anything, Vincent spoke through clenched teeth.

"I apologize that my being a man to you and Zion turned your life on its ear. That was never my intention."

"That's not what I meant, Vince," Imani tried to explain. "The only part of today that I don't regret was the time the three of us spent together. If you hadn't been here…"

"If I hadn't been here, some messy ass man wouldn't have run to Keith to tell him about us playing family. You wouldn't look like you've got a tennis ball in your jaw. Your neighbors wouldn't be in your business and neither would Child Protective Services. You don't think I've had plenty of time to think about all of this while I sat helplessly and watched the bullshit go down today?" he asked, his voice filled with guilt.

"Baby," Imani said, her heart hurting for him, "don't feel that way. If you hadn't been here, I never would've had the nerve to stand up to Keith the way I did. He's an idiot and would've found any reason to come over here and act like one."

For the first time, Imani acknowledged her situation by saying it aloud.

"And," she laughed softly, "when he saw this fine ass black man behind the door, he lost what little mind he had left. You see he didn't even try to swell up on you."

She laughed again, realizing Keith's cowardice. This time, Vincent laughed too, letting his defenses down.

"To be real with you, babe," she continued, "I'm not concerned with the custody battle that's definitely going to occur as a result of this. Between the police report, his arrest, the Social Worker, and his child support arrearage, I'm anxious to get before a judge. I have a friend who's an attorney and she's gonna eat him alive. I'm even looking forward to having that damn clause removed from the divorce decree altogether. Not that I need to," she paused, reaching and taking his hand, "because I don't see myself needing to, you know. Since you and I are going to be together, I won't be starting from scratch anymore."

That made Vincent smile. He liked the fact that she'd accepted him as a permanent fixture in her life. He'd felt like a failure by allowing her to be hit. Like if he'd moved a split second faster, he could've saved her. But he had to admit, the woman had chin. Most women would've been knocked completely unconscious by a lick like that. It hurt his heart to know her ability to take a hit like that was probably a matter of tolerance built up from years of abuse dating back way beyond Keith. He'd never asked, though. He didn't want to shake those trees. She'd been through enough tonight. He didn't want to do anything but help her relax and ease her fears about the next few months, and years, of her life.

"You know I'm going to be here with you through all of this, right?" he reassured her.

"Yes, baby," she said, her eyes never leaving the forest in front of her, "I know."

He sat and watched her smoke and sip her wine in deep thought. Her silhouette a bit distorted by the swelling, she was still a classic beauty. A majestic woman. She could be the future Mrs. Garvey. He smiled at that thought. Mrs. Imani Garvey…

What's Done in The Dark

Be careful when you pop in
You may be the one on the surprised end…
It's a shame…
I thought we had something worth workin' towards…

Imani ran her hands through her shoulder-length locs. She'd conceded after months of conversations with Vincent, and allowed him to start them for her. She was on her way to Atlanta for the first time since all the drama with Keith. With Nia giving birth to a beautiful baby girl that she'd named Akira, her child care had been non-existent. Vincent had come down as often as he could, but he'd acquired a contract with the Atlanta Health and Renewal Center, so he was busy juggling that and his personal clients.

She'd thought to call him and let him know she was coming but decided against it, choosing instead to surprise him. That, on top of the fact that their conversations had been kind of sparse over the last month or so. She'd attributed this to their schedules and her preparing for the custody hearing next week. That was part of the reason she'd decided to make the trip as well. Her attorney hadn't been able to get Vincent on the phone. Although they could've definitely made their case without him, between the police officers, Mrs. Armstrong, and his statement to the police, she couldn't imagine his not wanting to be there for her and Zion like he'd been all this time.

She took a CD from the visor CD holder and put it in the player. The writing on the disc read "Vincent Mix" and was a collection of songs that made her think of him. Everything from Anywhere by 112 to Prototype by Outkast to Fire & Desire by Rick James and Teena

Marie to Never by Jaheim. She smiled and grooved all the way up I-85. Ironically, she received a text from Prince Dawoud. She'd made it her business to limit interactions with him since she and Vincent had become so involved. Even so, his interest in her hadn't waned. And since it was Friday, she was almost certain the message was asking her if she was coming to town. Maybe she'd stop by and say hello on her way back to Montgomery. Maybe.

Imani smiled. She was proud of herself and her fidelity to Vincent, especially with the long distance. But he'd shown nothing but commitment and kindness to both her and Zion, so she figured the least she could be was loyal. Her phone rang. The Sistah ringtone from the movie The Color Purple, indicated that it was Nia calling.

"Hello?" Imani answered cheerfully.

"Hey Imani!" Nia matched her tone on the other end of the phone.

"Everything okay?" Imani asked the next logical question.

"Yeah, girl," Nia answered, "I just wanted to let you know that we got Zi from school and she's been such a huge help with Akira. She just changed her diaper and now she's sitting here feeding her a bottle. She'd make a great big sister."

"No ma'am," Imani stopped that conversation before it even got started, "this shop is closed for business. I get my Depo shot religiously every three months. Besides," she went on the explain, "between me and Vincent we have enough crumb snatchers."

She and Nia shared a laugh.

"Well, give Vincent my love and try to relax this weekend. Next week shouldn't cross your mind, okay," Nia instructed, knowing that her friend was going to worry regardless. Zion was her life and the thought of losing her had Imani worried to death.

"I'll try," Imani lied, knowing there was no chance of it.

"Mmmm hmmm. You know what Yoda says, you only do or not do. There is no try. Or something like that," Nia laughed, picking on Imani's love of Star Wars.

"Girl, bye!" Imani laughed, "Love you."

"I love you, too. Be safe," Nia said before ending the call.

Imani smiled from ear-to-ear. She loved her friend. Her life was almost too good to be true. She cruised, singing and smiling, all the way to Atlanta. She felt butterflies fluttering in her belly as she entered the city limits. She'd gotten there just in time to avoid rush hour traffic. The butterflies started to flutter more intently as she pulled up to the gate of the Country Club of the South.

This would be the first time she and Vincent had been alone in months. She loved the quality time they spent together with Zion, but she was limited with her screams of pleasure with Zion right across the hall.

The purple crotchless cat suit that she was wearing under her sundress was evidence of her readiness to get down to it as soon as Vincent opened the door.

She turned into his driveway, a bit surprised to see a Silver Kia Sportage parked there instead of his truck. She dismissed it, thinking he must've bought it for his daughter, Halle, who would be sixteen in a couple of weeks. She walked up the driveway and to the side of the house. She detached the magnet hide-a-key from the backside of the air conditioning unit. She walked back around to the front of the house and got her overnight bag and purse off the passenger seat of her car.

Imani unlocked the door, the alarm chirping her entrance, and laid the spare key on the table in the foyer. She was barely in the living room when she was startled by a young woman, who could've been her twin, except for her small, pregnant belly, who had a .22-calibur pistol pointed in her direction.

"Can I help you?" the woman asked from behind the gun. It was apparent that she'd noticed the resemblance, too.

"I'm looking for Vincent," Imani said, not moving an inch for fear of the young woman's trigger finger being itchy.

"He's not here. Who are you?" the woman asked, gun still pointed in Imani's direction.

"I'm Imani, I…" Imani started.

"Oh! HI!" The girl squealed, lowering the gun and rushing to give Imani a hug. "You're his sister, right? From Montgomery? It's so nice to finally meet you!"

She sat the gun down on the table beside the spare key. After an awkward embrace, she stepped back and introduced herself.

"I'm Saundra, Vincent's fiancée," she extended her hand to shake Imani's but it soon fell to her side when she saw the baffled look on her face.

"Are you okay?" Saundra asked Imani.

"No. I need to sit down," Imani said, feeling light-headed and short of breath.

"Sure," Saundra said, leading the way into the living room.

Imani followed her and sat down heavily on the sofa where she and Vincent had cuddled, made out, and made love several times. She looked at the Princess-cut diamond on Saundra's left ring finger. She looked at the slightly protruding belly the woman had out, wearing nothing but a sports bra and tights. She looked at the young woman whose face was almost a mirror reflection of her own, locs pulled into a ponytail on top of her head and falling around her face, brushing her shoulders.

Saundra could sense, from Imani's reaction, and her inspection of her, that something was wrong. She sat down, uncomfortably, in the rocking chair, leaning back and placing her arm protectively across her swollen belly.

"You're not his sister, are you?" Saundra offered, beginning what she knew was going to be an emotional conversation.

"No. I'm not," Imani responded, dryly. She wasn't sure whether she should be embarrassed or angry. She realized that she was a bit of both.

"Figures," Saundra said, reflecting Imani's expression, "I knew something didn't sit well with me. There are pictures of his ex-wife and kids, his sister Alecia and her family, but none of you."

She rubbed her belly. Imani felt like she was about to pass out because she'd lost her and Vincent's child.

"How long have y'all been together?" Imani asked, her throat dry. She felt as if the words were choking her on their way out of her mouth.

"Eight months," Saundra answered. "I'm a flight attendant, ya know. And I had my own crib 'til 'bout a mont' ago. My lease was up and, well," she patted her pregnant belly, "he said since we was gonna to start a family anyway, I might as well move in so he can be close to me and the baby every night. 'Bout that same time, he proposed."

Imani was taking in everything. Even the fact that their similarities stopped at their features. Saundra's speech was terrible. It made what she was hearing that much more difficult.

"Wow," Imani said in amazement, "I'm so sorry. I didn't know about you. I never would have…"

"It's cool," Saundra cut her off, "I knew somethin' was up. Too many thangs didn't make sense. I mean," she said shrugging, "it is what it is fa me, though. I had to quit my job because it's dangerous fa me to be in the air enough to make any real money so this is a real com'rtable situation for me, here, you know," Saundra stated her stance confidently.

"Yeah, I guess it is," Imani agreed.

"So, I ain't gonna trip. I just know what I'm dealin wit'. Now you," she looked Imani square in the face, "you look like you just got hit wit' a ton of bricks. I'm sure you got some words fa his ass and den some." She laughed to herself, "He on his way home so, if ya wanna wait for him, be my guest. But, say what ya need to and leave. We live in this gated community and I don't want no police at my door, ya get what I'm sayin?"

Imani nodded, debating whether or not she even wanted to confront Vincent at all. She was leaning towards just leaving without saying anything. Now, she was the one being studied. Saundra sat there, the obvious queen of this throne, rubbing her belly with her right hand, and twirling her engagement ring on her left. She was obviously trying to gauge Imani's level of crazy, waiting to see how much drama she was up for.

Imani let out a long sigh. She pushed herself up from the couch and walked to the foyer to collect her purse and overnight back from the floor where she'd dropped them when Saundra rushed her with the hug. She looked over at the gun on the table and decided it was definitely not worth it. She turned to look back at Saundra who'd gotten up from her seat and caught a pained look on the woman's face.

That confirmed for Imani that she hadn't been the first woman Saundra had had this conversation with. What's worse was that she was certain she wouldn't be the last. For a second, Imani pitied her. Then she was happy that she'd dodged this bullet, both literally and figuratively. She could, and would, definitely face Keith without Vincent if it meant avoiding this type of bullshit.

"Tell Vincent I came by," she requested, snapping Saundra out of her thoughts.

"I most shole will," Saundra promised, flashing a big smile.

Imani walked out of the house and got in the car. She called Prince Dawoud, who told her he was just closing up the shop and agreed to meet him for dinner at Pappaddeaux. She put the car in reverse and backed out of Vincent and Saundra's driveway.

She stopped at the stop sign as Vincent was turning onto the street. He slammed on the brakes at the sight of Imani's car leaving his street. His face looked like he'd seen a ghost. She raised her hand in a dismissive goodbye wave and pulled away from the stop sign. She was ready to get as far away from him as she could. At this very moment, she was happy he stayed so far away. She never had to see him again.

Pyramid

She was a walking tomb
Sporting the symbol of life around her neck
Yet death the only thing residing in her womb
Face painted to casket-ready standards
The ghosts of suitors past trail,
Hauntingly
Pall bearers…

While waiting for the gate to open to let her out of her living nightmare, she picked up the phone again and told Prince Dawoud she'd just meet him at the shop. She wasn't in the mood for conversation, just wanted a good dick beating to drive away the pain she was feeling. She needed to regain control, because between being lied to by Vincent and handled by Saundra, she felt like a punk. Nothing like a beautiful Rasta who'd been begging for her time and attention to rebuild her confidence.

When she pulled up to Little Five Points, she had her choice of parking because most of the shops had closed down for the night. She parked on the curb and walked to the end of the walkway and around the corner to Kloud Nine.

Prince Dawoud was standing shirtless, in a pair of brown linen pants, at the cash register. He had his back to the door and was busy rolling a blunt. When she opened the door, the hanging bell dinged her arrival. He greeted her with a smile and walked towards her, still rolling the green up in the Dutchess cigar. He gave Imani a hug so tight she could feel his heart beating against her chest. His chin rested on top of her head. They embraced for what felt like forever. Imani was surprised by how happy she was to see him.

"Come in," he said, once they had let go. "I see yuh ave locked it up, yeah?"

Imani smiled at his noticing his hair. "Yeah," she said, running her hands through it nervously.

"Nice," he smiled in approval.

Imani noticed for the first time that his teeth were slightly crowded on the bottom row. Her phone rang. She checked it, thinking it was Nia calling. When she saw Vincent's name on the caller ID, she put it back in her purse. She didn't have anything to say to him. Dawoud lit the tip of the blunt and pulled, blowing smoke into the air. The scent mingled with the Cocoa Mango smoke billowing from the incense sticks lit on the cashier counter. He must've seen the frustration in her face, because he walked over and placed his hand under her chin.

"You're too pretty to be bex, Sis," he said, looking her in the eyes so she knew he meant what he was saying.

"Bex?" Imani asked unsure of the word's meaning.

"Bingle, ah angry. Mad. Yuh ole face wrinkled up," he explained, offering her the blunt.

"Ohhh, vexed," she said, smiling.

She took it and puffed so hard she choked. This was an indulgence she'd picked up from Vincent. She'd already passed the drug test for the custody hearing so she didn't see the problem in joining him for one smoke. And it was definitely needed to calm her nerves from the encounter she'd just had not even an hour ago. She lifted her hands up over her head until her choking subsided and looked through teary eyes to see Dawoud amused.

She joined him in his laughter and they smoked and vibed off the reggae mix that was playing from the speaker box on the counter. Imani recognized a few of the songs, but the others were new to her. Regardless, they were all engrossing and, paired with the smoking, spoke to a deeper part of her being.

Redemption Song by Bob Marley came on. She passed the blunt back to Dawoud who held her hand longer than usual. Long enough to make her look up and see the sensual expression on his face. He took one more pull before placing the half-smoked blunt in the ashtray and pulling her to him. Lowering his head, he pressed his lips against hers and used his tongue to part her lips. Once her mouth was open, he blew a portion of the smoke that was in his mouth into hers. She inhaled deeply. They engaged in a fiery kiss. Smoke flowed from their nostrils like dragons and by the time it had all dissipated, their bodies had become steamy with the passion of kisses and hands traveling all over each other.

Sighs and moans filled the room, drowning out the music. Imani undid the tie on his lounge pants and he pulled her dress up and over her head. Both articles of clothing landed on the floor simultaneously. Shocked by the purple fishnet cat suit, Dawoud took a step back to admire the beauty that stood before him. She was so confident in her sexuality. She smiled as his dick jumped, betraying his mind and revealing his thoughts.

She was impressed by the length and the girth of it, even uncircumcised. She preferred not to allow an uncircumcised man inside of her, but tonight she was willing to make an exception. She motioned with her head for him to come to her. He eagerly obliged. He kissed her with a hunger and a passion that validated her sexiness to the nth degree.

He scooped her up in his arms and carried her to the back of the store where a futon sat upright against the wall. A red, green, black and yellow fleece blanket covered it, a huge print of Bob Marley's face on it.

Dawoud laid her down, breaking free from their kisses, trailing his lips down her neck. He licked and kissed her skin through the net material, making a bee line to her pelvis. He took full advantage of the opening, putting one leg up on his shoulder and pressing the other down slightly beneath his weight. He slid his hands into the sway of her back and elevated her pelvis so he could get full access to his meal of choice.

He took her entire clit into his mouth, pushed the hood back with his tongue, and hummed along with Peter Tosh's Vampire. The sensation made Imani shake. She sucked her teeth. Moaned loudly. She screeched and wiggled beneath his weight. He showed his strength, keeping her wiggling pelvis elevated so he could eat her until she couldn't cum anymore.

Imani, trapped, succumbed to his pleasing her. She let go of her need for control and allowed herself to be a woman, weak, and at the command of this man. She tangled her hands in his sandy locs and held on tightly for the ride. Imani, once again, reached a level of ecstasy she'd never achieved from oral sex. He manipulated her body with his lips, teeth, and tongue. She was a robot, responding to his oral coding. Her face twitched. Her eyes squeezed tight. Her stomach and thigh muscles jumped. Her toes curled. Combinations of his mouth movements caused curses to stream into the atmosphere from her gaping mouth. She gasped for air then choked on it.

After an hour of selflessness that left Imani weak, exhausted, and laying in a puddle of her own essence, he let her free of his grasp. He leaned back against the rail of the futon and looked at her with an expression that demanded her cheeks flush red beneath her dark brown skin. His hazel eyes had gone completely green and he looked like a beast with his locs falling into his face. Imani couldn't fight salivating at the sight of him. He grabbed himself with both of his large hands, pulling back his foreskin, revealing the large head that'd been peeking through at her. He waited for her to accept his invitation to give him head.

Imani crawled, cat-like, across the futon before taking a third of him into her mouth. He was a visual lover. Rather than rub her on the ass or tweak her nipples, he laid back and watched Imani maneuver him in and out of her mouth. He maintained a great deal of self-control, only letting out grunts and biting his bottom lip. His stoic face would've bothered Imani had his body not been giving away the true depths of his enjoyment. She felt his thighs tighten, release, retighten in unison with the tightening and releasing of her jaws. She swallowed him whole and released him from her throat's grasp.

His hands gripped the blanket and the futon cushion as he got more and more erect in her mouth. He grew solid as stone and throbbed his cumming, gagging Imani for the first time in her half-hour head session. She pushed him into her until his pubic hair tickled the top of her lip and held a strong, tight suction as he sprayed his soldiers down her throat.

He went limp, sliding like a recoiling snake back up her throat and into her mouth. Imani started sucking again, ready for another round, but he placed his large hands on either side of her face and pulled her head back until he was no longer in her mouth. Leaning forward, he laid her back onto the futon and peeled the cat suit off her body. He freed her breast, rolled it down over her waist, legs, and off her feet. He kissed every part of her, starting with her toes, up her calves to her knees, up her thighs and penetrated her with his tongue until she came again. He worked on up her body to her breasts, squeezing and suckling on them in a way that made Imani wish he had two mouths.

He regained his erection while rubbing himself against her warm, moist opening, but was obviously in no hurry to penetrate her. He licked up and sucked her neck until Imani was certain he'd left a mark. She was enjoying herself so much that she didn't give a damn. She just didn't want him to stop.

She reached down to put him inside of her. Dawoud grabbed her hands and pinned her to the futon. Without any hands, he navigated into her. Even though she was dripping wet, her walls were as tight as a vice and he had to work his way in. When he finally fit all of himself into the space of her, they both gasped loudly. He slow-stroked her until her eyes rolled back in her head and her walls clenched even tighter around him. He took this cue to push deeper and speed his stroke to a moderate tempo. Her moans reached an all-time high pitch and volume as he bumped up against her bottom. The sensation triggered his own release and he sprayed his seed deep within her.

They laid together, bodies covered in sweat. Chests heaving. He kissed her forehead before getting up and walking, naked, to the cashier counter to relight the blunt. He was at odds with his feelings. Imani could tell by his demeanor. She got up and crossed the room to kiss him and kick off round three. He pulled away from her and continued to smoke.

Now, Imani was the one with mixed emotions. His attitude was almost one of disgust. It was confusing to her and she didn't know whether she should collect her things and leave or if she wanted to stay and get to the bottom of things. She chose the latter. Walking back to the futon, she sat down and searched for her Blacks in her purse. She unwrapped one, pulled out her lighter and flicked it, holding the flame up against the cigar until the tip burned a bright orange.

"Dem deh tings will kill yuh," Prince Dawoud said to her, matter-of-factly.

"So will unprotected sex," Imani retorted.

"Indeed," he conceded, sitting down an arm's length away from her futon. His body language reeked of a mind filled with conflicting thoughts. "So, tell me, Sisteren," Prince Dawoud asked, "Why be suh reckless wid your life, den?"

He returned to her previous statement about unprotected sex.

"Why are you so reckless with yours?" she returned the challenge.

Prince Dawoud laughed, smoke bursting out of his mouth in big puffs.

"Calm down, Sis. I jus posed er question," he said, throwing his hands up in surrender.

Imani sat back sulking, feeling like he was mocking her. She could feel that he'd flipped into full judgmental mode.

"Yuh know what unsettles mi, Sis?" he asked rhetorically, "A beautiful ooman such as yaself, unawares of ya own power. When yuh walked inna dis store some months ago, I felt ya powa. Strong an prominent, a real lioness yuh were." He took another pull of his blunt.

"And now?" Imani asked interested, even though she knew it was going to hurt.

"Now, uh can't say uh know," he furrowed his brow in deep thought, "Yuh come hunreds of miles, dressed like yuh be, deny mi di pleasure of buying yuh a meal, an lay full open for mi to have my way wid ya."

Imani just listened. She was so tired of men having an issue with her willingness to have sex with them after they'd fucked her.

"I felt a chasm inna yuh. An openin gapin an wide. No fertile ground der atall. An I know fertile ground, I gat six chilren, myself," he looked at her, his eyes more brown than green now. He took another long, hard pull never taking his eyes from hers before continuing.

"Yuh practice cannibalism…"

"No the fuck I don't!" Imani interrupted.

"Yuh swallowed mi seed, Sisteren, human semen. Thousands of poss'ble human beins digestin in yuh belly right now," he explained. "An yuh uterus a wasteland. Place where men's seed go to die. You're a walkin tomb, baby gurl. The hurt deep in yuh cuttin off de promise a many, many men wid a machete."

Imani's eyes leaked tears into her bare lap. Frustrated, but unsure if it was with herself or with the truth that this stranger was telling her about herself, she got up and pulled on her sundress. She'd sort out her feelings on the drive home. Right then, she had to get the hell out of there.

As she put on her sandals and picked up her purse to leave, she didn't dare look him in the face. She didn't even bother collecting the cat suit, just left it crumpled on the floor where he'd dropped it. She felt more exposed at this moment than she had laying naked beneath him.

Imani walked swiftly to the door, only hearing bits of what he was saying about only wanting to help her begin healing. She snatched on the bar, trying to pull the door free. It took her a few snatches to realize that it was locked. She twisted the deadbolt and snatched the door open so hard that it knocked the bell from its cradle in the door jam.

She stomped away, realizing he hadn't even gotten up from his place on the futon. She was sure she'd given him quite a show trying to run away from the truth. She got into her car and sped through the streets of Atlanta, wanting nothing more than to leave this city that'd pulled the scabs off so many of her scars. She just wanted to get home. She knew though, that crossing the Alabama State Line wouldn't be able to save her from the internal bleeding. Her wounds were gushing and she knew she'd have to tend to them, not get a dick Band-Aid this time.

No one could love her in this state. No one would want to. She couldn't convince herself that she was just too much for them anymore. The reality was that she was wounded. Damaged. Broken. Her mind prisoner to the demons of her past. Her heart in a million shattered pieces, swept into a dustpan sitting within the corner of herself that she'd never taken the time to put back together. She'd been so busy with her extracurricular activities that she hadn't taken the time to repair herself. Her body was a heavy bag where too many men had come to pound away their frustrations.

She wasn't her own. And if she didn't belong to herself, how could she be arrogant enough to think she could honestly give herself to someone else? No wonder her love had been returned to her so many times unopened. The reality of it all made her head swim and her eyes overflow with tears.

Riding down I-85 South back to Montgomery, she wrapped her arm around her stomach thinking about the men she'd allowed to leave pieces of themselves inside of her. All of the one-night stands since her divorce. All of the men before marrying Keith. This was a sickening reality for her. So much so that Imani had to pull over to the side of the road and vomit. Once her stomach stopped turning with the painful reality of what she'd been calling life, she pulled herself back into her car and caught a glimpse of her paled face in the rearview mirror.

Who is this woman looking back at me? What is she? A whore? A jump off? A side piece? Imani couldn't even face herself and call herself a woman any man would be proud to call their own. She could be. But she couldn't say that she was at that moment.

She had no definition of self. No standards. No boundaries. Looking at herself right then, she knew she couldn't sell herself to a worthy candidate in five minutes, like she'd learned in her marketing class. All she had was pain. Dating back to before she even knew she was a girl. Had never been told she was beautiful, meaningful, memorable. She learned porn star tricks so that at least the men she sexed would remember her when their dicks got hard. Imani knew it was time.

Looking twenty-five in the face, she was halfway out of the second decade of her life with nothing but a child, a fading tan line on her ring finger, and good pussy with NASCAR mileage to show for it.

She reached into her bag sitting in her passenger seat, and pulled out the tattered composition notebook. This was her tally. Her little black book with names, dates, phone numbers at the time of the encounter, and grades for their performance. She told herself that she needed to keep track in case she came up pregnant or contracted something, so she would at least have an idea of who the culprit was. This was something she'd been doing since her first sexual encounter at fourteen. Now, eleven years later, she was more than one third of the way to Wilt Chamberlain numbers. Yep, he makes number 376. She made a mental note to list him in the tablet when she made it home safe.

She had to do better. Starting, her eyes shifted to her car radio clock and read 2:48AM today.

Imani flipped to a blank page in her notebook and turned on the ceiling light. She took the pen out of her hair, and began to write.

A woman is a portal to another world.

When she opens herself,

She is a pyramid, turned on its tip,

An opening capable of facilitating life.

But a woman, unaware of her power, could easily become a tomb.

Place where life water sits stagnant,

A festering puddle of her pain.

She...

Was a walking tomb...

Sporting the symbol of life around her neck

Yet death the only thing residing in her womb.

Face painted to casket ready standards,

The ghosts of suitors past trail,

hauntingly

as pall bearers to her self-inflicted doom…

It's Now or Never

It's time to face down my demons
No more running for me…
My Zi deserves a warrior…
And that, for her, I'll be.

The custody hearing was set for the Tuesday after Labor Day weekend. Imani had planned to spend the weekend preparing for the hearing and leaning on Vincent for strength. Now, she was left alone with all of these feelings swirling inside of her. She was grateful for Nia keeping Zion because her baby definitely didn't need to see her like this. She cried until she could barely see; her eyes were so swollen. She couldn't eat. Both the nervousness from the upcoming trial and her own emotional turmoil were taking their toll on her.

Every time she looked in the mirror, her scarred soul looked back at her. She couldn't sleep. Her dreams were too vivid. And now she remembered them in her waking hours. Wine didn't help. Blacks didn't help. And she had no interest in sex whatsoever. For two days and nights, she wrote, and cried, and wrote, and cried some more. Until she would pass out from exhaustion. On Monday night though, she prepared for the upcoming hearing. She bathed for the first time in days. Made herself eat some soup. Called Zion, who was having a blast at Nia's, and hearing her baby's voice dug up the little bit of strength she had left. She slept in Zion's bed that night. Smelling the mango butter oil that she custom made just for her daughter's hair.

Tuesday morning the sun beamed in, waking Imani before her alarm. She got up and ate a muffin and drank a cup of Chai tea. She collected all of her documents and sat them on the coffee table. She went upstairs and pulled out a hunter green business suit that she paired with a black blouse and two-inch black Mary Jane pumps. She put on light make-up and was grateful she didn't have large bags beneath her eyes from all of the crying she'd been doing. Looking at herself in the mirror, she saw a woman on a mission. A woman going to fight for her child. The epitome of a mother.

She grabbed her purse, her documents, and headed out the door. She and her attorney were going to meet early so they could go over everything. When she arrived at the Family Court Building on Mobile Highway, she saw Karrie, her attorney, waiting for her in the parking lot. She had an expression on her face that made Imani worry. Imani parked the car and walked up to Karrie, matching her concerned expression.

"What's wrong?" Imani asked, as they exchanged a hug.

"I didn't want to tell you this because I didn't want to rattle you," Karrie started, making Imani more and more nervous.

"What? Tell me!" Imani began to panic.

"Your mom and your Aunt are here…" Karrie explained, "with Keith."

"Say what?"

Imani was thrown off. She knew that her mother and aunt were upset with her for taking charge and choosing to be the constant in Zion's life, but she never would've expected them to side with the man they knew had abused her for years.

"Don't worry, their testimony won't hold any weight and I am prepared to handle them. I just need you to not come unglued when you walk in there and see them together, okay?" Karrie reassured Imani, followed by a genuine plea.

Imani took a deep breath. She was really catching it on all ends. She didn't think she could take much more. She went back to her car and smoked a Black & Mild, reminding herself that all of the evidence was in her favor.

"Damn you, Vincent," Imani cursed him aloud. He'd come and turned her life upside down and then gone and gotten another bitch pregnant. She'd never felt so alone.

As if he'd heard his name, Vincent's truck pulled into the parking lot, parking couple of spaces to the left of Imani. He got out and walked into the building in a crisp gray business suit, with a deep purple shirt and his locs in a neat braided style coiled, neatly on the back of his head. Watching him in the rearview mirror gave Imani butterflies. She was happy to see him and angry with him all at the same time. But now wasn't the time to be angry. She needed an ally and he was it. With him, Nia, Karrie, and Zion on her side, she would be just fine. Officers Timbres and Alexander pulled in next, parking in a spot reserved for police, and went into the Courthouse. Mrs. Armstrong came soon after.

Imani smiled. Her blood had betrayed her, but truth, right, and the authorities were on her side. She blew the last bit of smoke out of the cracked window before getting out of the car. She sprayed perfume on herself and entered the Courthouse. She walked through the metal detector and went into the waiting area. On one side of the room were her mother, Keith, her Aunt, and her baby sister, Shanna. On the other side, in a private room, Karrie was talking to the Officers, Mrs. Armstrong, and Vincent. When she walked in, she felt a pang of pain hit her in her chest, knocking the wind out of her. The sight of her family over there was seriously baffling. She shook it off though, and walked into the room with her attorney.

She didn't meet eyes with Vincent at all. He'd called and texted several times since seeing her leave his house, but she hadn't been interested in any explanations from him. He'd finally gotten the message. When Karrie was done explaining the way she would be calling the witnesses, she left to check and see how close they were to being called.

Imani got up to get some water and pee because her nerves were getting the best of her. Vincent followed. He didn't, however, take this opportunity to make his pleas. He walked up to her, getting close enough to her to invade her personal space.

"I'm here," he said, smiling at her.

"Thank you!" Imani said, full of emotion. She wrapped both of her arms around him and held on until her breathing calmed. She pushed back and looked at him embarrassed. "Thank you," she said again, under her breath.

"Jones. Keith Jones versus Imani Jones," the Bailiff called for her.

She looked back at Vincent lovingly and walked briskly back to the courtroom. When she, Karrie, Keith, and his attorney were in their seats, the door opened for the judge to enter the courtroom.

"ALL RISE!" the Bailiff ordered.

Karrie held Imani's hand on top of their desk as the judge walked in and the Bailiff read the list of rules for the hearing.

Well… here goes nothing, Imani thought. I get to take on all of the people who have hurt me at one time.

After The Pain

Life under a microscope
I can only hope that my truths were evident.
Too much time spent wallowing in the betrayal of
Loved ones with ill intent…

"Court is adjourned," Judge Watson slammed the gavel down.

"All rise," the Bailiff commanded.

Everyone in the courtroom rose as the Judge stood and exited the courtroom. Imani let out a deep breath once Keith and his attorney, the court reporter, and the Bailiff left the room. Karrie was still collecting her things and putting them into her briefcase. She felt like she'd been holding her breath the entire hearing. It'd taken all day to hear everyone's testimony. Even now, Imani was still reeling from it all. Her heart hurt. Her spirit was heavy. She had a migraine. She knew that part of the pain was due to hunger. She hadn't been able to eat anything when Judge Watson dismissed them for lunch. But that was a small part of it.

Most of her pain was due to hours and hours of testimony about her, about her life, about her flaws, about her inability to care for Zion. The worst of it didn't come from Keith, either. It was heart wrenching to hear her mother, her aunt, and her younger sister sit in front of her, and everyone else in the courtroom, and go on record saying things, some true and some flat out lies, about her.

Their words had cut her like a scalpel on an operating table. And that's what she felt like, a damned science experiment. She'd been under the microscope since the nonsense happened with Keith. Every aspect of her life was under a review. She was being chopped to pieces by loved ones. They spoke of her as if she was a stranger, like she'd heard them talk about others throughout her life. It had made her head spin when she realized why there were even there. If Keith got custody of Zion, which he really didn't want, she was almost certain that he'd agreed to sign custody over to her mother. This way he evaded child support, or so he thought. *You're such a fuckin idiot, Keith,* Imani had thought, cutting her eyes in his direction. *You really think that this woman, who is testifying against me, her own child, won't flip the script on your ass.*

The thought of them all conspiring against her, her family cutting a deal with the man who had beat her for the majority of their five-year marriage, made her sick to her stomach.

The entire trial, she'd had razor thin slices of her life, her personality, her promiscuous youth, her dropping out of college, severed. They'd been shoved down her throat and she had to sit there silently and take it. She'd taken the opportunity to recant all of their statements in her testimony. She hadn't harbored too long on disproving their every claims however, because Karrie had suggested that she make sure that it was known that her past, prior to Zion's birth, was irrelevant. Instead, they focused on the life that Imani had provided Zion, with or without Keith's help. Made sure that she wasn't penalized for being a single mother and had to work to make ends meet and provide a comfortable life for her child. Her testimony, unlike that of the others, was backed up by Vincent, Officers Timbres and Alexander, and Mrs. Armstrong. The fact that these were total strangers and unbiased, in addition to being officers of the court, gave their statements about Imani, Zion, and their observations that much more relevance.

What made her even more upset was the fact that this was just the initial hearing. Karrie had prepared Imani by letting her know that this could take months, even years, to be over. She would have to live every moment of her life as a model mother and citizen by the court's standards, in order not to give them any ammunition that could be used against her. She would have to allow Keith's visitation and as much as it pained her, she knew that he would probably use it to drop Zion off with her mother. That's the only way that they're going to see her though, because they know that they've definitely torn their asses with me, Imani fumed to herself as she and Karrie exited the courtroom.

"Are you alright?" Karrie asked her.

"Yeah, I'm fine," Imani lied. She smiled at the realization that Karrie had purposely taken so long to collect her things so that everyone else would have time to leave before they walked out.

"Thank you," Imani fought back tears.

"You're welcome," Karrie said, reaching for a hug, "you call me if you need to talk. And I'm not just talking about the case," she whispered softly into Imani's ear.

"Yes ma'am," Imani replied, trying her best to hold it together.

They stood there and hugged until Karrie felt Imani's breathing relax. They walked out of the Courthouse to a sun bidding their side of the world adieu for the day. As they walked towards their cars, Imani saw Keith, her mother, aunt, and sister hadn't left yet, either. They were standing under a tree across the parking lot, having a very in-depth conversation.

Imani felt the hair stand up on the back of her neck as she struggled to contain her anger and chose not to make eye contact with any of them. Instead she turned her attention to her car. She couldn't help but smile at the sight of Vincent, his tie loosened around his neck, leaning on the trunk of her car. She wanted to run to him and leap into his arms, but she managed to control herself. All but the broad smile that was spread all the way across her face.

"Well, lunch is no longer an option. How about dinner?" he asked when she was within earshot.

"I would love to," Imani accepted his offer.

"Let's both get out of these clothes," Vincent said, pausing to let the double meaning of his statement sink in, "and I'll come pick you up from your house in about an hour."

"Ok," Imani replied, stifling a giggle. Vincent still had her heart. Well, what was left of it.

She went home to change clothes and waited for him to arrive so that they could go to dinner. She wrestled with her emotions. Her frustration and anger with him. The terrible emotional roller coaster that she'd been taken on today. She had so much on her mind. But she needed closure. She needed to hear what the hell he had to say about Saundra and their unborn child. But, more than anything else, she needed someone to unload on or the hurt that she was feeling was going to eat her alive.

Imani heard three heavy knocks on the door. She opened it to find Vincent in a military green Ché Guevara tee shirt, camouflage pants, and tan Timberland boots. Ironically enough, she'd chosen to wear a camouflage maxi-dress with a brown half sweater and her high-heeled Timberland boots. Feeling rebellious, she'd even chosen to wear forest green lipstick.

"Let me go change," Imani offered, not wanting to go out looking like the cutesy couple that dressed alike when they went out.

"Absolutely not," Vincent dismissed the suggestion, "what you are wearing is too perfect for words."

Imani blushed and obediently picked her purse up from the table and followed Vincent to his motorcycle. She smiled because she'd hoped that he would drive his bike instead of his truck. She needed to feel free after being trapped in a room with all of her transgressions being thrown, like backhanded slaps, into her face all day.

She picked up the bottom portion of her dress and tied it in a knot so that it wouldn't be caught in the wheel of the motorcycle. Vincent handed her the spare helmet and they both got onto his motorcycle. She wrapped her arms around his chest and instantly felt safe. She laid her head into his back, smelling the incense and cloves of his hair and the cocoa butter through his shirt as they rode into the night.

Imani smiled as the wind whisked past them and her locs were pushed backwards off of her shoulders and flapped behind her from beneath the helmet. Vincent had been the first man to keep his word. Friend or lover, he'd been there for her, for Zion. If he wasn't the man for her, she would forever love him for teaching her what a good man should make her feel like. A woman. Strong and vulnerable. Passionate and beautiful. Loved, adored, desired. Never fearing being let down. Never settling for anything less than she knew she deserved.

Truth Be Told

Appearances can be deceiving
If self is already opened to deception.
Self-sabotage leads to posed questions
That have no place in love.

The motorcycle slowed to a halt. Vincent maneuvered it into a parking space adjacent to the entrance of the Olive Garden. It was a Tuesday night so business was slow, giving him his choice of parking spaces. He pushed down the kickstand and held his Gold Wing steady as Imani got off. She removed her helmet and shook her wind-tangled locs free. She untied the knot in the bottom of her maxi dress and rubbed the wrinkles out of the fabric. It was a nice night so she pulled off her short sweater, throwing it over her forearm, the lights from the parking lot making her seem to glow in the night.

Vincent sat still, enjoying her beauty. Even in moments as simple as this, she was breathtaking. He was grateful to be able to spend time in her presence again. He didn't spend too much time in admiration of her though, because he was on a mission. Getting off the bike, he removed his helmet and extended his hand in a motion that said, 'after you'. He knew that he was slightly taking advantage of her. If she weren't hurting, her mind and emotions all in disarray after the custody hearing today, he would've never gotten the chance to explain himself.

He'd been trying to call her since he'd seen her leaving his house last weekend, but she hadn't taken his calls or responded to his texts. He'd fought the urge to show up at her door because he knew she had enough to deal with in preparing to fight her ex-husband, Keith, for custody of Zion.

As they walked up to the door, helmets snuggled under their arms, he took a few swift steps so that he was far enough ahead of her to open the door for her. She smiled her thank you and walked up to the Hostess counter. He lagged behind a bit, this time watching her small frame and the way that the fabric of the maxi dress hugged and released her figure as she moved. Everything about her was perfect. From the toned back and shoulders, exposed by the razor cut of the dress' back, to her small waist, hips slightly spread from carrying a child, to her round, soft behind.

She turned from a conversation with the Hostess, Joy, a well-aging light-skinned woman with freckles and a perfectly tamed bob haircut sprinkled with silver strands. She giggled catching him admiring her.

"Vince," she asked calmly, trying not to embarrass him anymore than he'd already embarrassed himself. "Honey, I asked if you wanted a table, booth, or to sit at the bar."

Vincent walked swiftly to the Hostess counter and smiled at Imani and Joy.

"Booth, please," he responded.

Both women exchanged a glance and giggled.

"Follow me, please," Joy said, still giggling. She escorted the couple to a booth by the window and placed their menus on the table beside the green cloth-wrapped silverware.

"Your server will be Rachel. She'll be with you shortly," Joy announced. She shot Imani one more womanly glance, saying so much without saying anything at all, and returned to her post at the door.

"Enjoy the view?" Imani teased, trying to keep the mood light.

"Very much," Vincent said, his voice filled with sincerity. "Imani, I missed you so…"

"How are you guys doing tonight?" Rachel, a thick, brunette server with a round face full of life and gentle eyes greeted them, interrupting Vincent.

"We're doing well, thank you," Imani responded, happy for the interruption. She wasn't ready to hear Vincent's explanation just yet.

"Awesome! My name is Rachel and I'll be your server tonight. Would you all like to try a sample of our house wine, it's…"

"No, ma'am," Imani stopped her, "I would like a bottle of Lambrusco, please. Vince?"

She looked at him, waiting for him to place his drink order. She didn't mean to come across as rude, but she was in a hurry to get some alcohol in her system.

"I'll have a Peach Bellini Tea, please," Vincent ordered.

"And two glasses of water please, with light ice," Imani added.

"Coming right up," Rachel responded, "did you want to go ahead and place an appetizer order?" she hadn't missed a beat with Imani's cutting her off, much to Imani's relief.

"Yes, may we have the sampler?" Vincent asked, looking at Imani to see if she wanted something else.

She smiled her approval. A nervous smile that made her look like a child who had something to tell her parents that they knew would end in punishment. Vincent could tell that she was a ball of nerves. He hated to see her like this. It awakened his maleness. He wanted to fix it and was filled with frustration at the knowledge that there was nothing he could do.

His knowing that he was part of the cause filled him with even more guilt. He should've told her about Saundra but he hadn't known how. He never expected Imani to pop up at his house. They hadn't spoken in weeks, both of their schedules had been so hectic. Hers with the custody battle, work, and Zion. Him with his new contract, his regular patients, his family and, of course, Saundra and her pregnancy. He'd just gotten off the phone with her attorney, Karrie, when he turned onto his street and saw Imani sitting at the stop sign. Her face was filled with hurt and confusion. He'd been furious with Saundra when she'd told him what happened. He was becoming angry again just thinking about it.

Vincent took deep breaths to calm himself. He and Imani were both sitting there silently, caught up in their individual thoughts when Rachel returned with their drinks, the glasses of water, and their appetizer. His knowledge of the human body made him appreciate her ability to balance the large, circular brown tray between her shoulder, head, and neck. She sat it down on the stand and poured Imani a glass of wine. Placing the bottle back in the iced bucket, she placed their salad and breadsticks on the table and, at Imani's request grated almost an entire block of cheese on top of it.

They placed their orders, Vincent choosing the Chicken Marsala and Imani requesting the Steak Gorgonzola well done with extra Gorgonzola sauce. When Rachel walked away, Imani took Vincent's plate and filled it with salad. She pulled two breadsticks from their bowl and placed it on the side of the salad plate.

"Which of these would you like?" She asked, picking up another plate and motioning towards the appetizers sitting in the middle of the table.

"A little bit of everything, please," Vincent answered, watching in complete awe as she made his plates before she even thought to feed herself. This woman, he thought to himself with a smirk on his face, she's rare, indeed.

He knew that she was just doing what came naturally to her. However, she would spoil a man by just being herself. It bothered him that she was so unappreciated by so many. She placed the appetizer plate in front of him and began preparing her own food. Vincent seized the opportunity.

"Imani," he started, "I know what happened the other night when you came to see me."

"Do you, Vince?" she asked, never looking up from the task at hand.

"Yes," he responded, "I know that Saundra told you that we're engaged and the baby that she's carrying is mine. But…"

"Did she leave out the part about having a gun pointed at me? And why are you saying 'Saundra told me' as if what she said was untrue?" Imani asked, observing Vincent's choice of words.

"It's not true, Imani," he explained, "and what gun? There aren't any guns in my house."

Imani laughed aloud. Let the lies and bullshit commence, she thought to herself.

"You may wanna check under your fiancée's pillow when you get home, Hun," Imani said, her words shooting sarcastically from her mouth. "There was definitely a fuckin' gun pointed at me when I walked into your house last Friday."

She began stabbing at her salad and shoved a forkful of lettuce into her mouth. As she chewed, her eyes met Vincent's for the first time since their appetizer had been brought out. She looked at him, the shattered pieces of her heart shooting across the table at him.

Vincent chose his next words, knowing that she was in a very delicate state right now. Imani continued to eat, taking sips of her wine in between bites. After four or five bites, her wine glass was empty. She poured herself another.

"Imani, I'm so sorry," he spoke, his food sitting untouched in front of him on the table. If he couldn't get through to her, he knew he wouldn't be able to eat, sleep, or care to breathe again. He was in love with this woman and was pissed that Saundra had caused this drama. But, in reality, it was partially his fault for not telling her what was going on.

"Your food is getting cold," Imani pointed out, obviously trying to calm herself.

Vincent picked up his fork and began to eat obediently. The food had no flavor. He may as well have been chewing air. Imani was almost done with her appetizer and salad. Her second glass of wine was gone when Rachel brought out their entrees and a fresh batch of breadsticks.

"You're trying to make me fat with all this bread," Imani joked, "I'm gonna have to be rolled out of here at this rate."

"Honey, where do you think these hips came from?" Rachel joked back.

After grating cheese onto their food and clearing Imani's appetizer plate from the table, Rachel, who could obviously sense the tension between the two of them, took her leave.

"I'm gonna let y'all enjoy your meal, but I'll be close if you need me for anything, ok?" Rachel said on her way to the back of the restaurant.

As soon as she was out of earshot, Imani lit into Vincent. The wine had loosened her tongue enough to let him know exactly how she felt.

"I don't want a fuckin' apology, Vincent," she explained in a hushed tone. "I've been here before. But you could've let me know I was the sidepiece instead of feeding me all that shit about us being together. You met my child. This whole custody bullshit is because I let you in. Let you meet Zion before the six-month mark. If I'd kept you at bay, I would've found out about your Atlanta family and I wouldn't be fighting to keep my baby at home with me. If I hadn't been playing house with you, all out in public with Zion and shit, I... I..." she stuttered, beginning to get emotional.

"You would still be a slave to Keith and his shit," Vincent completed her statement. "You would still be cowering at the thought of confronting your mother... of protecting Zion from the same fate as you when you were a child. This was going to happen, Imani. Me being there was just the catalyst. What would've happened if Keith had come over there and jumped on you and no one had been there to stop him? Or worse, if one of your flings had been there and decided defending you wasn't worth it to him?"

Imani's eyes grew wide in her head. She wanted to scream. She wanted to throw her water in Vincent's face. He had some nerve.

"I would've made things right myself," Imani responded, her tone less hushed now.

"When?" Vincent asked, frustrated with her delusion.

"Eventually!" Imani answered, matter-of-factly.

"Bullshit," Vincent scoffed at her lying to him. To herself.

He cut into his chicken, never breaking eye contact. She was fuming. He sighed, knowing this wasn't what she needed right now and had certainly not been his intention.

"Imani, I was just the Universe's catalyst. You needed someone to be here with and for you when you were pushed into this inevitable situation," he spoke calmly. Rationally. He needed her to see past her anger, past the hurt. He needed her to see what was real.

"With me? For me?" Imani's frustration made her voice crack. "The Universe has a sick sense of humor then, got damnit. Send me a man with inability to commit, a fiancée and baby living with him while he comes to town and fucks me between visitations with the family he's already abandoned. I wonder if your lack of discernment with your dick was the reason your first marriage failed."

Vincent's chewing slowed. Imani knew how to hit a nerve.

He cleared his throat. "You do remember us having sex the night we met, right?" Vincent reminded her of how their first night together went.

"Oh, I remember," Imani responded, pouring another glass of Lambrusco, "I also happen to remember you being the one who took me to those cotton fields, which I'm almost certain you'd been to before. How many other women have you fucked out there?"

"I suppose a hotel room would've been more your speed, huh?" Vincent asked. "Or would I have been invited to share your bed sooner if I'd just been a one-night stand?" Vincent reminded her of her own indiscretions.

"Vince, I walked into your damned house and was greeted by a half-naked woman pointing a gun at me. I find out that you are engaged and have a child on the way but you want to talk about my shortcomings? I trusted you! And was betrayed during the time I needed you the most," Imani decided to express what was truly bothering her rather than continuing taking shots.

"Let's not even talk about trust. You kept your pregnancy with my child away from me. You let your punk ass ex-husband in to fuck and he left you and my child for dead. Thank God for Nia or my might have died and I would've been left in the dark. My own damn sister didn't even tell me. Can you imagine how that shit felt? And, all that aside, I was there today, Imani." Vincent reminded her, "and I'm here right now."

"Where is your fiancée while you're here with me?" Imani asked in between bites of her colding dinner.

"Imani," Vincent said through gritted teeth, "she's not my fiancée."

"Right," Imani responded, sarcastically, "she was just some lunatic, half-dressed in your house, claiming to be pregnant with your child."

"Why are you so quick to believe a complete stranger over me? If you really wanted to know what was going on, why didn't you stay until I got there or turn around when you saw me turning onto the street? I've been trying to call and have this conversation for days now."

He put a forkful of his chicken into his mouth, washing it down with a few sips of his tea. Imani was speechless. She had no answer. She remembered feeling punked and manipulated by Saundra when she left the house. She should've stayed.

"I honestly think you were looking for an out. I'm not afraid of commitment, you are. This felt too real to you. Too much like right and it scared the shit out of you. So you jumped on the first opportunity to bail that presented itself," Vincent slapped Imani in the face with his analysis of the events that led them here.

More silence. He was right and Imani knew it. She didn't have much to say. They ate in silence for quite some time. Rachel came to clear the plates out of their way and offered them dessert. Both declined.

"Take care of this whenever you're ready," Rachel laid their check on the end of the table.

Vincent reached into his back pocket and pulled his wallet out. He slid his credit card into the clear plastic slot in the check booklet. He motioned for Rachel to pick up his payment.

"Now, do you want me to tell you what's going on?" Vincent asked, grabbing Imani's hand around the remaining dishes on the table. "Or would you rather continue to make assumptions based on emotion and misinformation?"

"I'm listening," Imani prompted. She would listen, but that was all.

"No, you're not," Vincent said, a sad expression on his face, "you just say that you are. Your anger is blocking you from truly hearing me right now."

"Miss me with the psycho-babble bullshit, Vince," Imani said, disgustedly, "tell me what the business is with this girl who could pass for my twin walking around your house pregnant with a big ass rock on her finger."

"Well, first of all, the big ass rock on her finger," he reached into his jacket pocket and pulled out a black velvet box. He placed it softly on the table, "was for you. I was going to surprise you with it today after court. It's my way of showing you that I'm in this with you, and Zi, until death do us part."

Imani sat, frozen. Her large eyes were almost popping out of their sockets as she stared like a doe in headlights at the black box with Jared written on top in gold letters, sitting between them on the table.

"As for Saundra," Vincent said with a deep sigh, "she's a very troubled young woman. I grew up with her brother, Sam. He and I were close, best friends, actually."

His eyes welled up with tears. He sniffled loudly, pressing his thumb and index finger on alternating sides of his nose to stop the tears before they fell. This snapped Imani out of the shock. Her face contorted with care as she reached her other arm across the now empty table and offered her upright palm to him. Her body language asked him what was wrong but her lips couldn't process her thoughts well enough to allow her concerns to fill the space between them.

Vincent looked so sad and it frightened Imani. It made her that much more curious about who the hell this Saundra was. After a few moments, Vincent gathered himself and continued his explanation.

"You think you know someone…," his voice trailed off. He cleared his throat. "Sam… Saundra's brother was a good dude. He took care of their mother while she was dying from ovarian cancer. Gave up his teenage years to work and take care of Saundra once their mom passed," he paused, shaking his head. He was apparently having a difficult time processing things for himself.

"What is it, baby?" Imani coaxed, knowing that this was probably the first time he'd said any of this aloud to anyone. She set all of her feelings, all of her emotions, to the side and decided to be there for him. He was speaking of his friend Sam in the past tense. This led Imani to assume that he was dead.

"It's just hard, my love," Vincent said, holding her hands and looking her endearingly in the eyes. "See, he dropped out of school to work and take care of Saundra. He was really overprotective of her, to the point of whoopin' on her boyfriends and shit."

Imani nodded, wishing she'd had a protective big brother like Vincent was describing Sam to be.

"Well, that's natural, babe," Imani validated, "he was all she had left and vice versa, so he was just looking out for her."

"That's what we all thought," Vincent said, a darkness coming over his eyes, "until about three months ago when she called me asking if she could come stay with me. I knew Sam's wife, Alexis, didn't care for Saundra, but I thought it was because of her partying and the drug dealers and thugs she was always dating. It wasn't until she came over that night that I found out the real reason…"

Rachel coming to the table and returning their check interrupted Vincent. She let them know that the restaurant would be closing soon, but assured them that she wasn't trying to rush them. They nodded silently and neither of them spoke once she left. They broke their glance and Vincent wrote in her tip.

After he signed the receipt, they collected their things and walked back out to Vincent's motorcycle. Their pace and somber expressions resembled a funeral procession. It was unspoken that the conversation would continue once they were within the privacy of Imani's home. Vincent had motioned for her to get the ring box when they were preparing to leave the restaurant, so now it was in her pocket, the weight of it as heavy as the thoughts on her mind.

Time seemed to fly by on their way back to Montgomery. It was all a blur. When they arrived at her apartment complex, she suggested that they take a walk through Downtown to continue their conversation. Something about being trapped inside the walls of her home didn't sit right with her. And Imani knew, with all of the emotions they were both wrestling with, it wasn't a good idea to be in such close proximity to a bed, a couch, hell, even a table right now.

They walked halfway into Downtown Montgomery before either of them spoke. Vincent took the lead, seemingly eager to unload the burden he'd been carrying for months.

"Imani, what I was trying to explain," he began, his voice filled with urgency, "is that I found out that Saundra was pregnant and... the baby is Sam's."

He waited before continuing, allowing that tidbit to sink in. When Imani's face shifted to confusion from disgust, he continued, "Saundra and Alexis had apparently gotten into one of their many arguments and Saundra, in the heat of anger from being called a whore one time too many, had thrown in Alexis' face that her bastard was also her nephew," he explained, exasperation in his tone.

"What the hell are you telling me, Vincent?" Imani couldn't believe what she was hearing. She was filled with anger and frustration. She wanted to hug Vincent because the pain on his face was unmistakable. She wanted to hug Saundra, too. That poor girl, she thought, to lose your mother, suffer abuse at the hands of your brother, the only person you have left, then fight with his wife all the time and be carrying his child. Damn. It's a wonder she's still sane. Imani shuddered at how deeply their similarities ran.

Vincent had become silent. Imani reached out and took his hand. They walked silently together until they reached Court Square Fountain. Sitting down, side by side on its railed edge, Vincent looked at Imani longingly. His eyes showed pain and confusion. She saw, for the first time, that he needed her just as much as she needed him. But she knew from experience, that nothing good came from two damaged people leaning on one another. She stuck her hands in her pockets. Her left hand fondled the ring box. She really didn't know what to do at this moment so she decided to be present. Be there for him like he'd been for her today and so many times before. The rest, she would deal with when it came.

When she came out of her thoughts, Vincent had a face full of tears. He was so vulnerable, so open right now, and it shook Imani to the core.

"Gotta penny," she said, softly.

"I need a couple dollars' worth, baby," he said, his voice trembling.

She jokingly patted her chest, then her pockets. Reaching into her pocket, her hand slid across the ring box as she searched for her wallet. She pulled it out and removed her Visa card. She handed it to Vincent.

"Let's start a tab," she joked.

He burst into laughter, the light returning to his eyes for a few seconds before delving into the full story.

"When Saundra got to my house, she was a wreck. She told me that both Sam and Alexis had jumped on her. She was pretty fucked up. Eyes swollen. Lip busted. Hair all over her head. She was limping. Poor thing was all bloody and shit," he paused remembering the sight. "She was scared out of her mind. Didn't want to call the police. Even after her brother turned on her."

"More to cover his own ass and keep his secret," Imani seethed, getting angry with a man she didn't know.

"Exactly," Vincent agreed, "Saundra still refused to sell her brother out. She was overly apologetic, saying that she shouldn't have said what she'd said to Alexis."

"But, you got her to call the police, right?" Imani asked, wishing to accelerate the story to a happier place, if there was one.

"Yes," Vincent said, sadly, "they arrested Sam and Alexis for assault and battery. I think there's an attempted murder charge because of Saundra's pregnancy. They also charged Sam with the rape. Saundra, the poor thing, had nowhere to go so I let her stay with me," Vincent sighed again.

Imani knew that there was more. She reached over, resting her hand on his thigh. When he looked at her, she nodded her head, urging him to go on.

"She knew about you, baby," Vincent plead with Imani to believe him, "but the child has always had this obsession with me, ya know. I've always seen her as a little sister so I never entertained it as more than a crush on her big brother's friend."

Imani began to understand the situation a little bit more. That girl had been through so much. She wanted Vincent for herself and Imani had almost let her have him. She felt guilty not putting up more of a fight for the man she claimed to love.

It was quiet again as the reality sank in for both of them. Imani felt like this was a third chance for herself and Vincent. Vincent was just grateful to be able to set things straight with Imani. He loved her so much and thought he'd lost her.

Not wanting to risk losing another moment, Vincent slid off the seat and onto one knee.

"Imani," Vincent grabbed her hands and looked into her eyes, "I have known since the night I met you that you were special. I had no way of predicting that I would fall in love with you…," he stopped thoughtfully, "and Zion. I would love to spend the rest of my life with the two of you, offering the stability and happiness that the two of you deserve."

"Vincent," Imani stated, awestruck, "what are you saying right now? What are you doing?" She was alarmed. This day just got crazier and crazier by the minute.

"I'm asking you to pull that box out of your pocket so that I can do this right," Vincent said with a smile.

Imani freed her hand from his and stuck her hand into his jacket pocket. She ran her fingers across the box and froze. A man she'd told herself she never wanted to see again was proposing to her. What was she going to say? Was she ready to move to Atlanta, away from all of her friends, uproot Zion from everything she knew to be with Vincent? Was the story he just told her even true? I can check the arrests. They're public record, just have to get their last names, or maybe not, Imani thought, debating confirming what she'd been told.

"Imani," Vincent's voice jolted her from her thoughts.

She pulled out the ring box and handed it to him. Still on one knee, he eased the box open, revealing the ring once again in all of its two and a half carat Princess-cut beauty. It shone in the moonlight, entrancing Imani.

"Baby," he asked, "will you do me the honor of allowing me to be your husband and Zion's father for the rest of my life?"

Roller Coaster

Life's ride's twists and turns
Make my stomach churn and my head ache.
Reality filled with thrills and chills
Excites and sickens me.

Imani looked at her reflection in the mirror. Her dampened face stared back at her. Her skin was pale. Her eyes blood-shot. She'd spent the entire night vomiting. She knew part of it was nerves but had a feeling that there was more to her nausea than the custody battle, Vincent's proposal, and the stressful life she lived.

She looked at her left hand, the gorgeous diamond ring that Vincent had given her resting heavily on her middle finger. He'd left it with her until she made a decision. His disappointment in her not saying yes immediately had been apparent, but he understood that she had a lot to think about.

"God knows I wanted to say yes," she explained to her reflection.

She could literally see her heart and her mind wrestling behind her eyes. Love was so dangerous. So unfair. You couldn't help who you loved and this proved true with her family, Keith, and now Vincent. None of them were looking like anything positive. At least, that's what logic told her. But there's no true place for logic in matters of the heart and she loved each and every one of them in spite of herself.

Her stomach began to churn again. She felt sick and shifted back to her knees. She buried her face in the toilet. She'd thrown up all of the Olive Garden she'd eaten already, so there was nothing left on her stomach. This left her alternating between painful heaves that produced nothing and stomach acid that burned her throat, nostrils, and eyes on its way out.

When her stomach finally calmed itself, she laid her cheek on the cool porcelain of the bowl. She stayed there, afraid to move for fear of inciting another case of vomiting. Her mind was racing a thousand miles a minute, though.

I can't be pregnant. It's got to be stress and nerves. I missed my Depo shot appointment, but I got it as soon as I remembered. It's been so much going on, I lost track of everything. God, don't let me be pregnant... again... without a husband... again...

She lifted her left hand and looked at the ring. She sighed heavily, tears filling in her eyes. She just kept getting herself caught up.

What the fuck is wrong with me? she asked herself, getting frustrated.

It wasn't even an issue of the baby being Vincent's or her not wanting anymore children. It wasn't the fact that she was in the middle of fighting for custody of the child that she already had or all the drama Vincent had going on in Atlanta that was bothering her, either. It was the reality that, as careless as she'd been recently, she couldn't be sure that the baby was Vincent's.

Depending on how far along she was, Steve was definitely an option. She knew it was too soon for it to be Prince Dawoud's, but her uncertainty made her sick to her stomach. As her head swam and her stomach flipped, her phone rang. Fire & Desire, Vincent's ringtone. Imani wrestled with answering his call and ignoring him. She could say she was asleep in the morning because she knew if she answered the phone, he was going to insist that she let him come care for her. The way she was feeling, she probably wouldn't tell him no.

By the time she had managed to get up and drag herself to the phone, it had stopped ringing. Her phone chimed alerting that he'd left voicemail. Before she could click the icon to check the message, he called again.

"Hey baby," she answered, trying to sound as much like herself as possible, "I see you made it to your sister's safe and sound."

"Yes... I did," he said, something in his toned alarmed her.

"Baby, I know you're disappointed that I didn't give you an answer right away but..."

"No, that's not it," Vincent interrupted her, "Saundra just called and...," he sniffled loudly into the phone.

"What? What's wrong? Is she ok? Is the baby ok?" Imani forgot her own illness and became very concerned about this woman she'd only met once. Maybe it was just her nature because she didn't even have a reason to like Saundra after all of the drama she'd caused, and still seemed to be causing in her and Vincent's lives.

"Yeah, the baby's okat...," he confirmed, "but she's not. I just called the Alpharetta Police Department to confirm..." his voice trailed off, sending Imani into a panic.

"Confirm what?" she was screaming now.

How had this woman's life become so important to me all of a sudden? she wondered, she isn't, she told herself, I'm worried about my... fiancé. Just the thought of it made her smile. Calmed her a little bit.

"Baby, you're scaring me," she said, her voice shaking. "What's going on?"

Vincent sat on the other end of the line. He took a deep breath. Imani's concern meant the world to him. He decided not to upset her any more than he already had.

"Sam's dead, Imani," he explained.

"He's what?" she exclaimed, feeling herself getting queasy again.

"I got a call from my neighbor telling me he'd contacted the police because he had heard gun shots at my house. He knew I was here, so he didn't know who or what was going on. Then his wife reminded him that Saundra was there, alone and pregnant," he was filling her in on the sequence of events as briefly as he could so he didn't upset her anymore.

Imani could hear him gathering his things as he spoke. She knew he was preparing to return to Atlanta earlier than planned.

"And the police confirmed it was Sam who was shot? How the hell did he get in your house? I thought he was in jail," Imani posed what seemed like a million questions.

Her heart was thumping in her ears. She really didn't know how much more of this shit she could take.

"I guess he was out on bail," Vincent answered her thoughtfully. She was posing some great questions, it was almost as if she was speaking his thoughts aloud, kind of like his conscience. "I've been calling Saundra but I'm not getting an answer. I'm getting ready to head home and see what's what... Imani?"

Vincent heard the phone clatter to the floor and what sounded like Imani vomiting in the background. He found himself torn. Did he go home to find out what was going on at his house or rush to the aid of his future wife. Not going home right now could mean Saundra being arrested and spending the night in jail. It could also mean him being ejected from his community because these kinds of occurrences were frowned upon. They had rules about the length of your grass in the by-laws, he knew that this would be a violation of the Morals clause and the repercussions could be stiff.

But he'd just gotten Imani back. He could lose her forever by not being there for her right now. As he made the toughest decision he'd had to make since divorcing his ex-wife, he hung up the phone with

Imani in mid-hurl on the other end. He tied his bags to the back of his bike and hopped on. Alicia stood at the door, watching her brother crank up his motorcycle. She was in tears, wishing there was something she could do.

Vincent backed out of her driveway, giving her a long, solemn look before revving his engine and pulling off to the stop sign at the end of her block. He truly didn't know what to do. He sat there for quite some time debating whether to turn left towards Imani or right towards home and Saundra. Obligation weighed heavily on him from both directions.

When the car that had pulled up behind him blew its horn, he revved his engine once again before turning and speeding into the night.

****

Imani was awakened from her sleep on the bathroom floor by arms lifting her up. She thought she was either dead or dreaming because there was no one in the house but her. Nonetheless, she didn't struggle but chose to wrap her arms around her angel's neck and allowed herself to be carried into her bedroom and laid gently in her bed. It wasn't until she felt a cold towel pressed against her forehead, that she opened her eyes to find Vincent's forehead wrinkled in concern. That's becoming a common expression for him, she noticed. And it added years to his otherwise useful expression. She tried the best she could to smile.

"Why didn't you tell me you were ill," he asked, patting her face with the towel. He was so tender to her. She was so very happy to see him. She thought he'd left, headed to Atlanta to play Captain Save-A-Hoe to Saundra. He'd chosen instead to be there for her. That gesture meant so much to her. She wished she wasn't too weak to tell him, and show him, just how much. She slipped back out of consciousness, the image of him sitting on the side of her bed, squeezing the excess water from the rag in preparation of patting down her face and neck, sending her into the land of dreams.

****

Vincent lay in the bed, wide awake. Imani was resting calmly in his arms, her head nestled into the pillow of his chest hair, their legs tangled. He had too much on his mind to sleep. He was concerned for her health. She took precedence over the clusterfuck he had waiting on him at home. He'd spoken with the Detective on Saundra's case and explained that there were pressing matters that would prevent him from being able to return home tonight. Detective Rodriguez had informed him that Saundra had been released from custody because it appeared to be a case of self-defense. Even if she'd been held, she would've just had to spend the night in jail until he could get back.

Imani flinched in her sleep. He knew she was having one of her nightmares. He wrapped his arms tighter around her, hoping his presence would soothe some of her stress. It didn't. She flinched again before jerking away from him. She began writhing around in her sleep, her face tightening into the most horrifying expression. She mumbled loudly, words that he couldn't make out. Words that were accompanied by flailing arms and kicking legs. He jumped out of bed just as she flipped over onto her side and let out a chilling scream. He wanted to help her but he knew about night terrors and didn't dare wake her. He watched as she balled up into the fetal position in the center of the bed, face and body covered in sweat, and rocked herself into a better place.

When she finally stopped moving, he eased back into the bed. Imani crawled back onto him, in the same position she'd been in before. Her breathing was calm once again, and Vincent knew he'd made the right decision by coming to be with her.

Stuck Between A Rock & A Hard Place

I find myself torn
Between love and logic
Our dramas made for reality tv
We fight to be together in the midst of the chaos

Imani woke to the sun shining on her and a breeze blowing in from her bedroom window. The smell of turkey bacon and eggs made its way up the stairs. She smiled at the thought of Vincent in lounge pants, standing over her stove preparing breakfast. She sat up and felt light-headed because there was nothing on her stomach. She also had the urgency to pee. She scooted out of bed and slowly made her way to the bathroom. She went into her medicine cabinet to get the pregnancy test that she always kept on hand, and saw an empty space beside the box of Magnums on the shelf. Her slight panic was enhanced by her need to pee that she could no longer fight. As she turned to use the bathroom, she laughed at the sight of the EPT box sitting on the back of the commode. She opened the box and ripped the test stick free from its plastic wrapper. Pulling off the purple cap, she sat down and wet the cotton tip of the test.

Imani replaced the cap and laid the test flat on the back of the sink. She cleaned herself, flushed, and knowing that she had time to kill until the test rendered its results, she began to wash her face. She massaged Apricot face scrub into her skin, rinsed it clean, and patted her face dry. When she opened her eyes, she almost jumped out of her skin at the sight of Vincent standing behind her in the mirror.

"Baby, you scared the shit outta me," she exclaimed turning to face him, still refusing to look at the test's result.

"Is it mine?" he asked, very seriously.

Imani didn't take offense to this because her past and her own uncertainty wouldn't allow her to. She no longer needed to look at the test.

"More than likely, yes," she replied, choosing to be honest, "there was one other person before we became... exclusive. But that was a one-time deal and..." her explanation was stopped by him lifting her chin and leaning down to her ear.

"What you're saying doesn't matter, baby," he whispered. "Thank you for being honest, but that person growing inside of you is mine, regardless of what DNA may say."

He moved back and looked her in the eyes to make sure she got his meaning.

"Yes, Vincent," she corrected herself, mesmerized by the love in his eyes, "it's yours."

He pulled her close to him and she nestled her face into his chest. She smiled at the sound of his heart beating excitedly in his chest. Abruptly, she pulled back from him. She removed the engagement ring from her middle finger and held it out to him.

"Ask me again," she said, smiling.

Obediently, Vincent got down on his left knee and looked adoringly into her eyes.

"Imani Marie Jones, will you do me the honor of allowing me to be a husband, protector, supporter, and lover to you and a father to beautiful Zion and our unborn child, 'til death do us part?" he asked proudly, all the love he had for her filling his voice.

"Yes!" Imani squealed.

Vincent wrapped his arms around her, resting his cheek against her stomach. He couldn't think of any place in the world he'd rather be than right where he was. But he knew he was going to have to leave at some point to help Saundra out of the mess she'd gotten herself into, and he could only imagine what his house looked like with it being a crime scene now and all.

Imani felt his energy shift. She put her hands under his chin and lifted his face until he was looking directly into her own. She was loving the time with him, but knew he had business to handle.

"Baby," she said calmly, masking her disappointment, "you need to go."

"I need to be here with you," he retorted, fighting the obvious but knowing she was right.

She didn't respond, but her look said it all. She wasn't happy about it either, but she didn't want to make it any harder on him than she knew it already was.

"I've got Nia to help me and I'll call Alicia if I need to," she assured him, reminding him that she and his sister had forged a bond that had continued even after she'd cut ties with him behind the Saundra drama.

He got up painfully, his hands remaining on her belly. He kissed her forehead and led her to the bed so that she could lay down and eat. She dove into the plate of scrambled eggs, turkey bacon, grits, and toast like she hadn't eaten in weeks. He sat on the bed watching her, smiling quietly knowing that she wasn't just feeding herself, but their child as well.

Before he left, he washed the dishes, made sure she had plenty of ginger ale in her mini-fridge and saltines on her nightstand. So that she wouldn't have to get up, he placed a small, clean trash can on the side of her bed. By the time he was done getting her set up, she was drifting in and out of sleep. This made him want to snuggle beneath the covers with her rather than leave her there alone. But he knew that he needed to stop delaying dealing with the chaos and bullshit that was waiting on him. He reassured himself that he would be with her, Zi, and his unborn child soon enough and waited for her to open her eyes again so that he could tell her he was leaving.

She smiled a weak smile and puckered her lips, offering a kiss before he left. He set her alarm for three-thirty to wake her up and remind her to pick Zion up from Nia's a little later on. He left, feeling sadder than he ever had any time they'd parted.

The drive home for him was almost unbearable. The scenery he usually enjoyed when riding his motorcycle, just served as a reminder of the amount of distance that stood between him and Imani. The two and a half hours felt like an eternity.

When he arrived at the gate of his community, he felt light-headed as he punched in the code for entry. His heart was racing and he felt like he hadn't taken a breath in half an hour. He crept through his neighborhood, feeling as if all of his neighbors were peeking through their blinds in disdain. He felt like the wind was knocked out of him when he turned on his street. His house was covered with yellow crime scene ribbon. His door sealed shut with neon orange tape.

It dawned on him that he couldn't go inside of his own home. Had no access to his things. Couldn't shower or sit on his furniture or, even worse, couldn't assess the damage and see what was still intact, what was destroyed, and where the blood was. He made a U-turn in the cul-de-sac and headed towards the police station. At some point, he was going to have to track Saundra down. Right now he wanted to know how long he was going to be kept away from his home and get as much information as he could about what happened.

To be continued...

Stay tuned to find out what happens with Imani and Vincent. Does she retain custody of Zion? Does Vincent lose everything, including

Imani, trying to clean up Saundra's mess? And find out what's been up with Tammy and Tyrone from Side Piece Chronicles after Imani saved Tammy from Tre…

Made in the USA
Columbia, SC
22 October 2023

24446296R00130

WHEN
SILENCE IS
GOLDEN

SAYING NOTHING
MAY MEAN *EVERYTHING*

JERMILA SEALYS
Foreword by **Allison Hermia Tench**